Knight's Fork

By Seth Jamieson

Samadhi and my family told me I could do it

Preface

Dear Citizens,

In response to a freedom of information request made by a St Wilfred's Secondary School Student, for their project on modern politics in The Republic of Yorkshire, the following personal accounts have been released to the public.

All Yorkshire citizens are required, by law, to keep a diary in which they pledge the honest truth has been recorded. This was implemented in 2091 on the basis of the Reliable Witness and Justice Act introduced by the Yorkshire Independence party. This Act was written into law due to the shocking lies and false accounts given in court by pro-UK activists after the revolution. To make sure accounts in future were accurate, all citizens must be willing to swear in court that their diary records are true. The following accounts are provided for the student's benefit and include only elements pertinent to the time frame and the individuals named in the request.

North Yorkshire County Council would like to take this opportunity to emphasize that these accounts are personal and liable to individual opinions which may not be reflective of the truth in its entirety. Furthermore, writing styles may vary and disagreements between accounts are still possible. Some accounts are obviously written with the reader in mind whereas others are written in a personal reflective style. The accounts provided have not been edited and only minor omissions have been made within the dates requested.

We hope these accounts are used wisely and treated with the respect they deserve.

Your ever faithful servants,

North Yorkshire County Council

I, Kaley Abrahams, present this account as part of the appendix to my History Research Project discussing politics in North Yorkshire at the turn of the 22nd century. I have made no alterations to the words themselves although I have added chapter headings as I felt appropriate and removed dates to make it flow like a story. I have also removed some of the extended accounts which were not related to politics in North Yorkshire. I hope you, the examiner, find this interesting.

Chapter One: Narcissism

I, Jonathan Malenkovic, of sound mind and body declare the following account to be true. I will hold back no thought or deed which could paint me in a different light than that which I deserve. Of you, I ask only one thing, reserve your judgement until the story is complete. Remember, all men are flawed, some are just more open about it.

Sat in the pub with my home friends on holiday from university, I sit in thoughtful silence and muse. What would I do as North Yorkshire First Minister? I would probably make all my friends cabinet ministers and host celebrity parties in Castle Howard. I would definitely impose bank holidays with no discernable reason to celebrate. I would rule with an iron fist and yet be loved and respected. All in all, I would be a First Minister to be remembered. I would work with the other three First Ministers and give them whatever they want so long as I have a nice life in my mansion. I can just say to the public that I am promoting harmony and cooperation.

The path to the North Yorkshire throne is dangerous but fast. First up, I need a seat on the county council and that requires beating one of the permanent members. Rowan Schofield is the newest member of the council and, since no one has seen him play chess, my best bet. He had gained his seat through a deal with a family friend who resigned to him in a bid to avoid being defeated, and subsequently executed, after his diagnosis of dementia. He had chosen Rowan as a challenger and so no one has actually seen him compete.

"Rowan is surely my best bet," I exclaimed around the table at my local pub. It is Christmas and my former school friends have reconvened for a booze-up and a chat; James has just turned twenty giving us an excuse for a get-together. We are in Harrogate, the capital of North Yorkshire, in a pub developed from the remnants of an abandoned train station. High arched walls and fancy staircases give the illusion of grandeur, but this is a pub for those whose conversations were not worth overhearing and whose aspirations rarely amount to anything. I am hoping to put an end to that trend.

"If you can take a seat on the council, execute Rowan and establish a following in the county. You will be duelling the First Minister by June! At least that's what Katherine Tyne did…" exclaimed Ollie, a politics undergraduate at Huddersfield with an excitable personality. I like to keep him around

9

despite his lack of contact with reality. He gives my ego a boost every so often. Talk about a brown noser. His time scale is off, but his premise is correct, nonetheless. As soon as you take a step up the ladder, the top isn't so far.

Grace is not so enthusiastic about my plan, but no surprise there. She has been jealous of me ever since we met in primary school. She is the classic example of what happens when you are constantly coming second. Bitter, flakey and depressed. The terrible triad. One particular occasion comes to mind, playing draughts in year 9 (chess is reserved for the sixth form and above due to the severe consequences of duelling) she had flipped the table in anger when I reduced her to two pieces. She had come crawling back to me and I accepted her apology, but just because her festering resentment amused me for the rest of my school days. If I were to become First Minister I think she would flee the country.

James is wandering back from the bar now, pint sloshing from side to side, threatening the brim with each clunky step. He sits down with a thump, shifts in his chair and splutters,

"Let's face it mate, you may be good enough to play these council prunes, even good enough to beat them but you don't have the nerve to cope with the pressure! Have you ever even played under full dueling rules?"

"No, but I have played with a lot at stake!"

"Betting your student loan is not the be-all and end-all. You could have got a job or begged your parents for money." I hear a little snigger from someone at the table. "Playing chess with the threat of death in the background is on another level."

There is no one who can sour your mood quite like James. James is one of those people who doesn't excel in knowledge but has wisdom beyond his years. He does lack a bit of tact though and will tell you straight, whenever, wherever and with whomever nearby. He had cost me a girlfriend back in year 11 when he told me to stop talking about her behind her back. He said this while she was in the room! You can trust him though; he is a good friend when you need him.

"Alright mate," I reply, "Let's have a game, if you win, I will submit myself to the executioner. If I win, you come with me to challenge Rowan and act as my side kick."

"That's not the same pressure though is it! If I win, I am not going to demand your death and you
11

know it. That's just not the same." He makes a fair point.

"Yeah, but you could do in theory and if you win, I will know for sure that I can't challenge Rowan." I argue.

"Fine, it's your funeral." He says this just before taking an enormous gulp of beer.

James pulls out his ancient smartphone and boots up the government chess app to check the rules. He entered the terms of our duel and I sign the consent form. If I lose, he has the right to demand my death within 48 hours of the game, if he loses, nothing happens.

James has had a few pints, so I am not really worried. He also sucks at chess, he had to re-sit his duelling exam in lower sixth form.

Sure enough, the games a joke and I beat him in 22 moves.

"I am a man of my word; I will come with you to the duel. Let's go to the courthouse and challenge him tomorrow."

"Ok, well I am gonna hit the hay then, we have no idea how good Rowan is, sleep is important. I could still beat him with a hangover though, I reckon. Better safe than sorry for now." I am a little taken aback that I am suddenly challenging Rowan Schofield tomorrow. Can't back down now though.

Chapter Two: Chess Dueling

The Geniocracy system was designed for people like me. History lectures in Skipton have drilled this into me. In 1977 Raël, a French journalist turned religious leader, proposed that a minimum level of intelligence should be ensured before someone could run for parliament. The Yorkshire Nationalist party had taken this one step further. They extended Raël's idea after witnessing countless incompetent governments rule over England. The leader of Yorkshire was to be an excellent strategist, well-educated and calm under pressure.

But this was not enough. The people of Yorkshire were also tired of bored private school graduates wreaking havoc in the political system and then leaving without any repercussions. To become the leader of Yorkshire, you have to risk everything you have for your beliefs. With this in mind, the chess duelling system was developed and eaten up by the citizens of Yorkshire.

The principle was simple. Chess is a game which encompasses strategy, experience, knowledge and sacrifice. It is one of the only games in the world where both sides are almost exactly equal. Of course, white has a slight advantage but only a perfect computerized system could really take advantage of this.

All school children are given the same amount of education on how to play chess, no discrepancies, no discrimination, no disadvantage. In fact, following the revolution, it became illegal to offer private chess tuition or teach others online. Learning the game by yourself showed ambition and determination. With this in mind you can buy books on chess. Strange distinction in my mind but there you go. They claimed that leaving some children less educated than others would mean great potential and intelligence would be lost and Yorkshire would be worse off for it.

Finally, the Yorkshire Nationalist Party needed a system to discourage random duelling by any loser with aspirations and increase the pressure on the game. The death penalty was reinstated for duelling only, not even murder could invoke such a severe penalty. Before each game, both participants have implicitly agreed to the Yorkshire government rules. You cannot duel and subsequently claim you don't understand the rules. There are some possible variations, you can offer money or work instead of your life. All payments must be offered within 48 hours or officials would enforce them. Any challenge to a government official must be played on pain of death. The death sentence is carried out immediately.

There are exceptions, of course, exceptions prove the rule. If you play chess in the presence of a lawyer, then you can negotiate a truce during the game and agree a winner with different implications. This is how Rowan Scofield took the old council cretin's seat on the North Yorkshire County Council although that was engineered by the old codger before the lawyer got involved.

All schools in Yorkshire were teach the chess curriculum from sixth form onwards. You can officially challenge someone to a duel at the age of 16. Government officials attend each lesson to ensure everyone has the same level of teaching and the entire curriculum is covered. Chess has become a way of life with many civil disputes settled at the chessboard rather than in court. It is vital that everyone knows how to play to a certain level; failing the end of school exam requires a compulsory re-sit.

The system has become more nuanced through the years. There are more aspects to intelligence than just the ability to play chess; social intelligence, linguistic intelligence and self-awareness are just a few components of intelligence not reflected on the 64 square board. It is amazing how much of lectures you remember when you test yourself. See what I mean, intelligence like mine is wasted in Skipton. It is unsurprising, therefore, that skilled communicators have since persuaded chess players to play on their behalf. Many companies have employed chess departments to deal with their legal issues as it is faster than taking someone to court. This was a stroke of genius, the company is not liable to death you see, the individual chess player is.

Major disputes between companies have ended up in wars of attrition, picking off each other's chess players until the CEO could be challenged directly. Thirty years ago, this was common practice but since then the great chess players have cottoned on and realised they were being treated like pawns. To hire a company chess player these days would cost you a fortune. Imagine the life insurance.

With the salary of professional chess players increasing by the day and the number of duels taking place reducing by the year, a career in chess has never been more enticing. When I was in school, people would sneak recording devices into the chess lessons to relisten later. Any advantage over everyone else could be life-changing, not to mention lifesaving. Luckily, I had the natural talent to dismiss all those schemers.

I had been offered a position to study politics in York on the back of my chess report and my mathematical ability but the border skirmishes had rendered the universities' credibility perilous and so I settled for the post-revolutionary University in Skipton. In hindsight this was a mistake, I am too good for Skipton and should be in Castle Howard running this pathetic county. Even Ollie in Huddersfield is having a better educational experience than me. What a waste, trying to educate Ollie is like trying to teaching a fish to ride a bike. My aspiration-less parents had insisted I stay in North Yorkshire, still living under the delusion that the four counties are all equal.

I should have applied to West Yorkshire, almost every successful chess player graduated from Leeds, Huddersfield or Bradford. Obviously, South Yorkshire has its occasional genius through Sheffield University and since the East took York from North Yorkshire they have been on the up and up. Parental obsession with North Yorkshire could ruin my life, fortunately only idiots want to run North Yorkshire so I will still make it to government. Governor of North Yorkshire is a cushy job, all the perks of a council leader and no pressure from the uneducated citizens to improve anything.

It's 9:45 and I am still in bed although I am revising basic chess strategy so I'm not being lazy. James messaged me to say he was on his way to the courthouse to offer the duel on my behalf and countersign as my representative. He should be here soon with the official government receipt of a challenge accepted. Rowan has to accept but gets to decide when we play within a fortnight.

I move on from the basic chess strategy revision to planning my policies for my first year in local government. I need to toe the line enough so that I will not be held responsible for any policies which insight challenges from individual angry constituents. Furthermore, I will need to go under the radar until I have had time to establish a challenge for the North Yorkshire 'throne.'

"Johnathan Malenkovic!" A booming voice echoes through the hallway, "When you are having friends over you must give me some prior warning, I am still in my dressing gown!"

I take a deep breath; my goodness does my mum irritate me in the morning. I roll out of bed. James is stood bolt upright by the front door, clearly uncomfortable with the commotion he has caused

19

by just turning up. He looks me in the eye, and I can sense his relief at not having to make small talk with my parents any longer.

"You got it?" I ask briskly.

"Got what?" Interjects my mum. I had not told her my intentions.

"Yeah, he accepted for this afternoon. We have to be at Castle Howard for 4:00 pm." James attempts to pass the duelling receipt to me, but my mum snatches it out of his hand and looks at it in horror.

"Are you out of your mind? My son! What are you doing? Why would you put your life at risk? Why didn't you discuss this with your father and me?" She is on the verge of wailing. I can't tell if she is feeling anger, disappointment or sorrow. Tears are streaming down her cheeks and she is glowering at James as if he is partly responsible.

"Mum, calm down," I say in my soothing voice which has proven effective in the past. "I am challenging Rowan, he is rubbish at chess, and then you will have a son on the local council! It will be fine from here on out, no more worrying about me after today."

"Are you actually insane? No one has ever seen councillor Schofield play; he could be incredible, and I have seen you play. You are good son, but you have not got enough experience to challenge a politician. You could have waited!" She is having verbal diarrhoea.

"Well, Rowan has accepted, and I have made up my mind. I will win mum. I will make us comfortable for the rest of our lives."

"I am calling your father right now." Mum storms off into the kitchen, believing that my Dad will convince me when she has been unable to.

James looks at me in astonishment. I don't think the little weasel has ever been so uncomfortable. The kid clearly doesn't know what to do with his hands. He is constantly flickering between crossing them and putting them behind his back.

"You didn't tell your parents?" He looks at me in disbelief. I just look patronizingly back at him. This was not the big deal they were making it into. Once I win, I will lord it over them. My parents will be grovelling to me for money and special governmental favours. Every time they ask, I will subtly remind them that they didn't believe in me.

Chapter Three: The Duel

Castle Howard is meant to be the setting of all duels with the penalty of death in North Yorkshire, but it is technically legitimate to play anywhere. It is preferential nonetheless as the executioner's office is in the outbuildings which makes the duels enforceable. There is also a film crew as people like to bet on some duels, especially when a county councilor is challenged.

James and I enter through the main gate and are greeted by a cluster of journalists in the main courtyard. There is a bustle of journalists talking in hushed tones whilst glancing at the schedule on the wall with the duels for today. A tall cameraman walks up to us and looks befuddled.

"Are you the young guy who is challenging Councilor Schofield?" He asked James. "John Mal…en…kovic?" He hasn't looked at us once, he is looking at a long list of names on his phone.

"No that's me." I make a point of looking him in the eye with an air of derision.

"Cool, let me just get Amanda." He says this as he is already walking away.

"He didn't even ask us if we wanted to speak to the press!" James says quietly. James has no idea how politics works. Of course, I want to speak to the press, I am about to become a politician, the people need to hear my voice, see how confident I am in the face of this duel. A tall woman with flowing brown hair approaches us, I recognize her from the TV. She is beautiful, there is no other word for it. She swivels around to face the camera in front of us.

"We are joined by the first challenger of Councilor Schofield. John Malenkovic is a 20-year-old, Skipton college student with grand ambitions of government office. Tell us Mr Malenkovic, what made you decide to challenge councillor Schofield?" She turns her face slightly, so she could still be seen on camera, and propelled her microphone into my face. I am blown away by how beautiful she is.

"Rowan Schofield has been letting us down ever since he took office! Let me ask your viewers, what he has done for any of the people of North Yorkshire?" I declare with the air of a 21st-century politician.

"You mean aside from his work with the homeless in Scarborough, the legislation making severe depression and anxiety a disability and securing the move of Coca-Cola to Knaresborough from Wakefield?" She is looking at me as if I am deluded. I don't know whether it is because she was pretty or because I had made a mistake but instead of answering her retort, I just stare at her. She seems charmed by my good looks and then turns to give the camera her full attention.

"Well, an interesting duel this afternoon with the popular councillor Schofield being challenged by this idealistic young man who clearly believes Schofield's efforts to improve North Yorkshire are falling short of what is needed."

The cameraman lowers the camera, and the famous journalist turns to us with a more relaxed expression. She looks me up and down and then smiles. "It was nice to meet you, good luck in the next life." With that, she walks away. What a nerve! She'll regret that when I am in power. She will get no stories from me ever again.

James is looking increasingly disgruntled. "I want you to beat him now just to prove all these nay-sayers wrong."

"Wait you didn't want me to win before?"

"I didn't want you to play him at all. I was hoping someone, or something would persuade you out of
24

this." James stalks away, ashamed that I have exposed him for his doubting. He said he wanted me to win to prove the nay-sayers wrong, but he is just another nay-sayer. The hypocrisy.

The journalists aren't interested in us anymore. Some powerplant official is talking about a worker's rights issue that they are going to settle at the chessboard. We walk through the courtyard and enter Castle Howard. We are welcomed by a noticeboard, not even a receptionist, just a noticeboard telling us where to sit in the hall. We are 15 minutes early so James and I sit in the reception on some sofas which look more comfortable than they actually are.

James is fidgeting in his seat. First, he would do up his top button and then undo it again. Then he begins tapping his fingers on each other in a methodical order. Finally, he is repeatedly touching the tip of his nose and then adjusting his glasses. He is making me nervous, and I was not nervous before. I start asking him questions about what he would have done if he was First Minister. This seems to calm him down. He gives me some drivel about funding mental health research and improving the infrastructure system between the major cities of North Yorkshire. That took his mind off it and made me feel more like a politician. He believes I was listening to him, that's basically all a politician needs to do. Pretend to listen and then appease.

A team of men and women dressed in suits walk by briskly. I spot a small pistol strapped to the leg of a thin woman. She is clad in all black and has a white rose imprinted on her dress. She walks with an incredibly straight posture and is accompanies a bespectacled man with wrinkles marking his temples. I recognize Rowan Schofield, but he looks more distinguished and qualified in person. He has extensive stubble and is wearing a tight blue suit. He doesn't even glance in my direction, he continues to chat with his aids as they walk to our chess table. He takes a seat but continues to talk with his team. He doesn't acknowledge the white and black armies on the table in front of him.

"I guess that's my cue." I stand up and James looks nauseated as he drags himself to his feet. We wander to the table. My heart is pounding, my mouth is dry, I am glad I wore a suit jacket as my armpits are soaked through. I sit down with an air of confidence and look Rowan Schofield straight in the face. This is my time, this is my game, this is my destiny.

Chapter Four: The Art of Surrender

The despicable man continued talking to his lousy associates until an official approaches the table to start our chess clocks. Ninety minutes each. Schofield was to start but he continues talking to his team. Fine by me, waste his own time on the clock. Eventually, the striking woman with the white rose on her dress nudged Schofield and motions with her eyes towards the chessboard. If I thought Amanda Buckle, the journalist, was impressive this lady blows her completely out of the water. Schofield turns in his chair, looks at me, and then moves his king's pawn forward two squares.

The opening salvo passes in silence. Neither of us has lost any pieces but Schofield clearly has control of the centre of the board. I position my queen with pride. My defence is settled, time to attack. Schofield sits back in his chair and surveys his options. Nothing will happen imminently, time to intimidate this buffoon.

"I bet you regret not taking me seriously now." I try to say with an air of smugness, but it comes out with more anger than I anticipated.

"How old are you, young man?" He replies cooly.

"Don't try and demean me. Our system means intelligence prevails; age doesn't matter."

"Intelligence prevails in theory; wisdom prevails in practice. There is a reason employers want work experience on your CV." Schofield crosses his arms as he says this and glances back at the board. He obsessively adjusts his glasses. If someone counted I think he touches them at least every minute. I take the cue and look towards the game as well. All of a sudden, Schofield's pieces seem to have aged, they are peering down on my pawns with derision. They are exasperated at my stupidity.

"When I am on the council, I won't be chatting rubbish about experience, I will be ruling with an iron fist and living in comfort." I say to distract from a sudden gush of panic stirring in my soul. Panic is for the weak, I will not let it show.

"Oh, I see." The edges of Schofield's mouth curve upwards before a smile bursts out across his face. He makes a moderate attempt to conceal his glee.

His stubble makes him look friendly on TV but up close it is more threatening and masculine.

"You see what?" For some reason, my voice betrays my internal anxiety.

"You are an awful person." As Schofield says this, conveying utter certainty, the camera crew in the chess hall move closer towards the table. I bet all the TV channels will be showing this exchange on the news later. This is a key moment politically; I will win this game, but I also need to win public approval and exchanges like this will be watched all over the county. I need a strong comeback, but I am distracted by Schofield's henchmen. The woman in the black dress is just looking at her phone. Her boss is going to die today, why doesn't she care?

Before I have time to reply, Schofield makes his move. It is a devastating blow. Moving my queen from the back row left a pawn defenceless. It is a rookie mistake. Schofield moves his knight into the gap, placing me in check but simultaneously in a position to take my rook. It is known as a knight's fork and I should never have let it happen.

"Check." He bellows. The camera must be able to see my dismay as it is being moved closer to my face.

Schofield turns around and restarts his conversation with his team in hushed tones. I can't make out what he is saying. I can't make out anything. My collar has become tighter around my neck, my lip is trembling, and I am no longer convinced my suit jacket is disguising my sweating anymore. I move my king out of check. Schofield glances back at the board and takes my rook. He turns away again. I may have lost a power piece, but I am not down and out, especially as he is not paying proper attention.

I move my queen into a threatening position and glare defiantly at the man who holds my life in his hands. The story is not over yet. I am smart enough to get out of this. I feel a bead of sweat run down my trunk from my armpit. Schofield turns back to the board again. He raises his eyebrows; I have his respect once more. I deserve this man's respect; my previous panic is being replaced with pure rage.

He starts laughing. He is laughing out loud at my move. The woman looks up from her phone and glances at the board. She lets out a snort of derision and returns to analysing her phone. Anger is burning through my mind, destroying villages of neurons on its path. Every thought, every idea is clouded by anger. My synapses no longer transmit information, just rage. However, one thought breaks through.

I have made another mistake. There is no way back now. Realistically, it is over.

Schofield leans over the table and catches my eye deliberately. He takes my queen with his bishop and then throws my piece across the room. The camera crew follows it through the air where it hits the floor and bounces around the walls in the corner. The chess hall has a stone floor making the bounces sound like humiliation.

"Do you concede, or do you want to drag this out?" I am a rook and a queen down; I have taken none of his pieces and I have no power pieces in the centre of the board. I have lost. Instead of answering his question, I continue to play as if he had never asked anything. I may as well continue; these could be the last few seconds of my life.

"Nevermind." He moves his second knight. It's checkmate. I didn't even see that coming, he was asking me to concede to preserve my dignity. It was a test.

The smartly dressed government official of the chess hall walks over and declares Schofield to be the victor. She places a pistol on the table and walks away. Her hair is in a ponytail and I feel a woosh of cold air fan my face as she passes. I watch in a daze. James watches from afar. I can hear his phone buzzing from across the room, probably my Mum messaging him frantically as she watches from home. My Dad will be so disappointed. Grace will be loving this.

Schofield clicks his fingers to get my attention. I watch on as he gets up. He doesn't pick up the gun! He begins walking away. The camera crew turns to follow him. I am off the hook. He has granted me mercy; I am humiliated but alive.

The striking woman stands up quickly and half walks half runs towards Schofield. She grabs his arm and whispers in his ear. He walks back to the table.

His voice is loud, and his words are cutting. "You challenged me for no reason. You just wanted power, fame and money. You do not care about the people of this county. You only care about yourself. If you had challenged me because you had ideas, because you wanted to help your people or because I had grieved you, I would have let you live. Narcissists like you don't deserve to live on. If I let you live, you could challenge one of my colleagues, even take their place and destroy everything we have achieved for this county." I divert my gaze.

"Rosanna."

The woman picked up the gun on the table. She looked me in the eyes, she winked. The last thing I am able to record, she winked. I write this last entry in the executioner's office of the outhouse in Castle Howard. I would like to thank my family and friends for the life I have had. I pray that someone will read this someday and see Schofield for the scumbag that he is.

Chapter Five: A Second Perspective

I, Rowan Scofield, Black Square Rook of North Yorkshire County Council, declare the following account to be honest and true. In all aspects I will recount, to the best of my knowledge and ability, the events and thoughts which take place in my mind. I ask that you do your utmost to understand my perspective, even if you disagree with my motives.

As I walk into Castle Howard, Rosanna and Callum give me a compact lecture on the difficulties the welfare system is experiencing following severe anxiety and depression being classified as a disability. Apparently, hundreds of employees across North Yorkshire are leaving their jobs and taking up a benefit cheque in its place. As I enter the courtyard Callum shows me a viral clip of the Scarborough jobcentre with citizens queuing around the corner.

A cluster of excitable journalists spot us in the courtyard and run whilst breathlessly shouting into their microphones. We slightly increase our pace and manage to enter the reception area of Castle Howard with only a few screamed questions reaching our ears. We storm through reception, deep in conversation.

"You need to reconvene the council, Rowan. You need to persuade them not to repeal the disability definition. Claire and Esther are already campaigning for the repeal; declaring that the definition will cause economic instability. The videos from today are only strengthening their argument. We need some damage limitation." Rosanna is wearing her duelling dress; the Yorkshire rose emblazoned on her chest. She understands politics better than I do and yet she never bothered to learn chess seriously. She always wears her Yorkshire rose when a duel might affect our position in government. However, this is the first time I have been challenged directly.

Callum runs to catch up with us. "You're on table 14. I will notify the official that we are here. Have you seen this trumped-up kid challenging you? He is sat in reception pretending to discuss politics with his friend. If he is not even listening to his friends, why does he want to represent the whole of North Yorkshire?"

I shrug my shoulders and find my seat. Rosanna is still thinking about defending our legislation. "Look Rosanna, you may as well start messaging councillors to set up meetings. I could fit Katherine in this afternoon I'm sure, and she is the pivotal vote."

"Sure thing, Rowan."

The kid has arrived, and the clocks have started. Rosanna nudges my arm and gestures towards the chessboard. I open with the napoleon attack and within the opening set up, I know this kid is useless at chess. He seems happy not to have lost any pieces and is ignoring the gaping holes in his defence. He makes a confident attacking move; I admire his ignorance. It is meant to be bliss after all. Today his ignorance will be exposed, however, and for that I pity him.

I sit back in my chair and try to weigh this young man up in my mind. He is well dressed but visibly nervous, his collar is drenched in sweat. He seems innocent enough, maybe he is challenging me because his home life is terrible, and he wants to change the fortunes of his family. Or maybe he is challenging me because he wants to do more for people with mental health problems. Maybe his parents have recently lost their jobs and he believes I am responsible.

My train of thought is cut short by a torrent of arrogance from the young man's mouth. "I bet you regret not taking me seriously now." He splutters with contempt. I give him the benefit of the doubt. He may have figured out he has made a mistake, and this is just a sign of how nervous he is.

"How old are you, young man?" I try to say this as reassuringly as I can. Hopefully, he will realise that I am on his side and will have mercy on him. That question is my invitation to walk away. He is dressed in a light blue shirt with a loosely fitting suit jacket. He still has some remnants of acne breaking through the skin on his face.

"Don't try and demean me. Our system means intelligence prevails; age doesn't matter." Comes the reply. He insulted me! I gave him a chance, and he insulted me in return. He must not have seen his mistake. This teenager thinks he is smarter than me. If he was to win, this adolescent would kill me without hesitation. He loathes me for no discernable reason.

"Intelligence prevails in theory; wisdom prevails in practice. There is a reason employers want work experience on your CV." I say casually.

He wails another ignorant insult and I relent to acknowledge his arrogance. "Oh, I see," I return to our game. My clock is still running after all. "You are a horrible person," I move my knight into the gap. Malenkovic may as well be spitting feathers he is so angry. His cheeks are bright red with rage.

"Check." I declare. This idiot has wasted enough of my time. I return my attention to Rosanna. "Have you heard back from Katherine?"

"Nothing from her but Anthony is available this afternoon."

"Anthony is spineless, is there any point meeting him? He will change his mind depending on what the majority is voting for around the council table."

The arrogant young man has moved his king out of check. I take the rook without much thought. Callum is adamant that any meeting with a councillor is a good sign.

"If you meet with Anthony then the others will know you are serious about continuing this policy and will be willing to listen to your ideas. Trust me; Meet with Anthony." Callum is a social person. His specialist area of expertise is persuading people. Trusting him is always a good idea.

I return to the chessboard and am baffled with what I am greeted by. Not only is his queen in a terrible position, undefended and takeable but the boy is looking at me dead in the face with an element of defiance in his expression. I start laughing, I can't help it. What makes it even funnier is that every second of laughter makes the sweaty teenager angrier. Even Rosanna can't resist letting out a snort of laughter and she barely plays chess.

The boy's rage turns to panic. He has spotted his mistake. He looks as white as a sheet and is desperately evaluating every possible move he can make once I have taken his queen. I know he is wanting to continue. He is desperate for power; he is desperate to kill me. I take his queen and throw it across the room, the camera crew love that. It is a symbol; I am showing him it is over. His words are the only thing that can save him now. I want to let him live.

The chess hall is massive and the clinking of the queen in the corner echoes through the hall. It is a very humiliating noise for the poor kid. I notice a whisp of facial hair growing on his lip. He is so young! What is he doing here?

"Do you concede, or do you want to drag this out?" If he didn't catch my earlier offer for the

39

preservation of his dignity, surely, he will see this one. It is checkmate in one move after all. To my disbelief, he pitifully moves a pawn forward, a completely irrelevant pawn to the route of my potential checkmate. The word, "never-mind," slips out of my mouth.

Callum beckons the government official over and she declares the game over. She places a pistol on the table in front of me. She walks away. Must be common practice for her. The act of execution means nothing to her anymore, just part of the job. Well, killing someone is not normal for me. I am not a monster. I am not a soldier. I am just a flawed man, trying to do the best for my people. John Malenkovic is one of my citizens. Is he not someone I am meant to represent and protect? I snap my fingers to get the kid's attention, he is away with the fairies understandably. His previously perfectly gelled hair is not disheveled and covering his forehead.

I hope this display of compassion will change his life for the better. Maybe he will reflect on this day, the day I let him live. I get up and walk away. In my peripheral vision, I see Malenkovic's relief.

Rosanna is at my side in a flash. "You have to execute him. Not only is he one of the few who actually deserve capital punishment, if you let him go, every man and his dog will think they can challenge you with no repercussions. Remember councillor Trinity, he granted clemency to his first challenger. He had thirty challenges in six months after that. Politically speaking, you must perform your governmental duty."

She is right, as always. I am not a killer though and Malenkovic's whisp of facial hair is playing on my mind. Rosanna is more than a political mastermind but today she has a new job description including the phrase: Henchwoman.

I return to the table and see the minimal colour that had returned to Malenkovic's face drain out of it again. I check to see the camera is at a good distance, it is a little far away, so I speak up.

"You challenged me for no reason. You just wanted power, fame and money. You do not care about the people of this county. You only care about yourself. If you had challenged me because you had ideas, because you wanted to help your people or because I had grieved you, I would have let you live. Narcissists like you don't deserve to live on. If I let you live, you could challenge one of my colleagues, even take their place and destroy everything we have achieved for this county." The am thinking of reasons as I speak, I feel a little more justified in my decision. Although, let's face it, I just listened to Rosanna without debating it.

The poor young man cannot look me in the eye. His friend watches on from the back of the room. He can see what is coming, everyone can see what is coming. Rosanna has picked up the gun silently. "Rosanna." Saying her name is enough.

The official calls security and I cannot bear to watch them drag him across the courtyard to the executioner's office. I leave that duty to Rosanna. Callum and I move on. Time to meet Anthony. I feel awful.

Chapter Six: The Emergence of Rowan

"You could have been more intimidating in your speech!" Rosanna is miffed. "You basically said it was ok to challenge you so long as you want to change something or have practically any morals." She did not take long to perform the execution and is back at my side in no time. Rosanna is a very empathetic woman really; it is a strange how little emotion it takes for her to put the geniocracy system into practice.

"Rosanna, people are more likely to challenge a councillor who they see as callous and mean than one they respect as honourable. If another 20-year-old arrogant boy wanted to challenge me I am sure the image of you picking up that gun will put them off."

"But what about the professional chess player at a major firm who believes he deserves an easier life?" She asserts.

"Then he will challenge a councillor who is either morally corrupt or bad at chess. Let's face it,

Anthony probably won't make it to the New Year." I deflect.

"Well, let's hope you live to tell the tale." This is one of my favourite things about Rosanna. She believes that there is no way of knowing anything until it has come to pass. She willingly accepts that she might be wrong and yet spends her life trying to be right. That is true wisdom. Wisdom in Yorkshire always prevails. Rosanna is not anywhere near as tall as people think she is. She wears enormous heals in public but when she sits down you can see the discrepancy. She only takes those shoes off when we are back at the Octagon.

As we leave Castle Howard, an array of jubilant journalists want to ask me if I 'have blood on my hands.' So unoriginal. They ask every politician that after a fatal duel. The media is often anti-capital punishment until a senior government official gets executed and then they say they can't admire the system more if they tried. Aside from the one journalist who jumps out in front of the car door and calls me a coward for not pulling the trigger myself, we leave uneventfully. One second they are appalled that someone has died, the next they are appalled that the politician didn't pull the trigger themselves. They can't have it both ways.

In the car, Callum has yet more viral videos to show me. These, however, are in our favour. A young man with crippling agoraphobia has mentioned me by name on his video channel. He calls me a voice for the oppressed and says they have finally been able to get financial support to seek the counselling he so desperately needs.

"Can you get this video on the news tonight?" I ask Rosanna, she has a lot of connections.

"I'll give the Stray Ferret a call," Rosanna says, ever my knight in shining armour.

"We need to move the queues around the job centres from the front pages to the back. And Callum, make a compilation of videos from people with legitimate mental health problems who support our definition."

"Aye aye, captain."

It's 4:45 and we are 40 minutes away from my office in Harrogate. Harrogate was once a town, in the days of the United Kingdom. Since the revolution, it has become a major hub of activity with its close vicinity to Leeds and being the largest populated area of North Yorkshire. Ripon, formerly a city was stripped of its title. It was made a city by the Queen of England in 1836 because of

45

its Minister which was converted to a Cathedral for no apparent reason. With so few people in Ripon and so many in Harrogate, the titles were reversed with Harrogate inevitably going one step further and becoming the capital city of North Yorkshire.

Nevertheless, Harrogate's importance remains directly correlated with Leeds. All roads lead to Rome. North Yorkshire is, to all intense and purposes, dependent on the pity of West Yorkshire. The only exports from North Yorkshire which exceed imports are water (Harrogate Spa water continues to be a well-established brand), rhubarb and Coca-Cola since I managed to secure their interest in a factory in Knaresborough to replace their factory in Wakefield. A move with which West Yorkshire took extreme offence and have been subtly punishing us forever since.

My office is in an apartment block called the Octagon, a poor pun based on the Pentagon in the United States of America, which overlooks the *Valley Gardens*. It was left to me by councillor Stewart. Councilor Stewart has been a family friend ever since I was little. He went to York University with my Mother. I have a feeling it would do me some good to record this story again now, to re-emphasize why I went into politics. I did not join the council to kill people university graduates with ambitions! Around this time last year, in the dead of night, he called me and asked me to come to the Octagon.

"North Yorkshire is being treated like gum on a shoe." Councilor Stewart had mused as he sat on an armchair with his back to a small fireplace. I was sat across from him on what can only be described as a cushioned stool. In all the years I had known him, I had never felt so inferior. He stood up and moved the chessboard into the corner of the room. "I am not the man to change that fact."

"Yes, you are. You have been on the council for thirty years. If you make a statement, people will listen, things will change, you are the key to North Yorkshire's future. You can be the spark that lights the fire." I replied, out of friendship more than anything else.

"I am the spark; you are correct about that. But this spark will only light the match. It is the match's responsibility to start the flame."

"What are you talking about?" He always spoke like this with me, strange metaphors.

"Rowan, you are the match, I am the spark, and the people are the fire." He looked at me with an intensity I was unprepared for. "I am old, and I am
47

burned out. You are young and you are passionate."

I stood up from the stool. We stood in the room together. No longer family friends but comrades in arms. I had been waiting for my opportunity and was quite literally jumping at the chance. "Every revolution starts with an idea. Our idea: North Yorkshire should be the controlling state of Yorkshire." Councilor Stewart smiled for the first time that night. In hindsight I was a little too eager, might have offended him a little and should have given him more flattery before accepting.

"Here's the plan. I am in my 60s, I am going to leak to the press that I have been diagnosed with dementia. I will declare that I have been challenged by a young man called Schofield and instead of playing the duel we have agreed in private that you will take my seat in return for allowing me to live on as a citizen of this great county."

"You have dementia?"

"No, I don't have dementia! Cheeky Sod. You'll need to wise up when you're in office." He was laughing now and had returned to his armchair. "One piece of advice, the road that lies ahead of you is long and precarious. You need to find an issue which is important to the people of North Yorkshire but that is neglected by the central government. You need to be seen as the legitimate voice of the people in the face of oppression and selfishness."

"Mental Health." I say without hesitation.

"Bingo."

We arrive back at the Octagon. I fling my keys into the bowl and carefully place my suit jacket on the hook behind the door. "Beer?" I ask generally to the room.

"Whisky," Rosanna answers absently, she is glaring at some email from someone who I should probably care about for some reason or another.

"None for me, Paul has arranged a date night. I'll see you bright and early in the morning." Callum hadn't even come in the room and was hovering in the doorway.

"Tell Paul he is a lucky man." I wink as I say this. I find it funny making Callum a little uncomfortable.

"Let's hope he still thinks that!" Retorts Callum as he closes the door behind him, ignoring my fake flirting.

I have updated the décor of the Octagon since I inherited it. The only remnant of Stewart's days is his armchair, I have repositioned that in my office. It serves as a reminder that I have a legacy to live up to. Rosanna has poured herself a drink and is sat on a bar stool by the kitchen island. She has not poured me a drink. Anthony is due in thirty minutes.

Chapter Seven: The North Yorkshire County Council

Anthony is the epitome of everything I hate about modern politics. He is a smart man, to be on the council you have to prove that, but he remains on the council by holding no views. No one cares about him, so no one challenges him. He is always on the side of the majority. He never speaks first; he is a sheep. Well, I want to lead this lamb to the slaughter.

He enters my office with an air of superiority. He surveys Rosanna as he walks in. "Looks like you relished the opportunity to kill that man today." He says this with a sinister creepy old man vibe.

"Let's hope you never have to play Councilor Schofield. I will enjoy shooting you more." Rosanna spits the words at him in disgust. This is not how I would normally like an important meeting to start. Anthony is a short, fat, bald man with a thin mustache. He is dressed in a pinstripe suit and genuinely looks like a crook. He wears pointed shoes that Roald Dahl would have commented on as the sign of a witch.

Anthony makes an exasperated snorting noise and turns to me for support against Rosanna. I am not falling into that trap, so I gesture for him to take a seat, it is a non-cushioned stool, to make him feel even more uncomfortable than I did when I was invited here last year. Within seconds of sitting, I can tell how unpleasant the seat is, it is very enjoyable for the viewer.

"Mental health reform, how do you think it's going?" A nice open question, good to assess the lay of the land.

"There are some positive developments, but the economic situation is concerning." He says this with an air of contemplation. He is pretending he didn't know what this meeting was about and that he is simply reflecting in the moment. I turn the TV on.

The Main Headlines today, (Amanda Buckle, the news presenter, is in Rosanna's pocket.)

Huge swathes of anxious and depressed North Yorkshire citizens have praised the county council for backing their request for financial support. Here is a clip.

52

I turn the TV off before they start talking about the welfare system and turn to Anthony once more.

"Sounds like the citizens like the reforms. Tell me about your economic concerns." This puts him on the spot. He readjusts his tie as he tries to remember the spiel he had prepared on his way over.

"I have seen some footage of the jobcentre in Scarborough and there are reports of similar numbers of people are asking for support at Richmond's welfare department." He seems excessively proud of himself for making a mildly pertinent point.

"That is a very legitimate question and I understand your concern," that'll boost his ego, "I would, however, beseech you to look to the long term."

"Always the best idea," Rosanna shouts from the kitchen, takes a sip of her whisky and then resumes her email extravaganza.

I continue, "The short-term picture, I admit, is complicated. There will be transition changes and patches we need to iron out. There will be many people who attempt to claim benefits, but fear not, the GPs will refuse to describe them as seriously

53

unwell and their claims will be rejected." He seems receptive and attentive, but he is not interested in the arguments themselves, he is interested to see how persuasive I can be. If he thinks I can persuade the rest of the council I am sure he will back me.

"The long-term implications are the most important aspect of this legislation. Last year there were 30,000 sick days for mental health illnesses. Only beaten by days off for headache and back pain. Think of how significant that is. Now, with a disability definition like our legislation, the central government is forced to supply research funding to our universities and, I am assured, we have a good chance of developing an effective treatment for anxiety and depression, so long as we can secure the funding for the foreseeable future."

"And who says we are close to this breakthrough?" He still isn't sat comfortably and looks tiny beneath me. I can see residual hairs on his head, determined to grow despite the overwhelming balding.

"Professor Odoi." I always like name dropping famous academics.

"You spoke with Professor Odoi? He hates politicians." His disbelief amuses me.

"He hates bad politicians! He was willing to speak with me." I boast.

"If that is true, he only spoke with you because you were offering him money. All scientists tell you they are close to a breakthrough if you are sat with your cheque book on the table."

"You are showing your age there, I have never used cheque books." He did not appreciate this jibe and his lack of smile only made his wrinkles more visible and his hair greyer. "Professor Odoi has proven his academic integrity many times over, I am sure the council will find his proclamation very convincing." The wrinkled old man shifted on his uncomfortable stool and rearranged his legs so that they stretch towards me.

"I agree, and I must admit I am hopeful for a future where depression and anxiety are a thing of the past. Imagine the efficiency of a workforce without stress." He is lying, he couldn't care less about people's mental health.

"Well, we would not exploit our own, would we Anthony?" He laughs it off, but I don't buy his comment as a joke. "Can I count on your vote tomorrow?"

"Let's see what the council have to say, but I'll tell you this, you are a convincing young man and I have every confidence that you can persuade the others." What a slimy man. Why bother meeting me at all if you have nothing to discuss? I smile and thank him for his time, Rosanna curses him under her breath as he puts his coat on in the kitchen. As he leaves, he tips his hat to her; she jumps upright and curtseys with extreme exaggeration. Anthony leaves as he entered, exasperated and uncomfortable around Rosanna.

"I have heard from most of the council members. They seem to have discussed it among themselves and say anything you have to say you can say to all of them tomorrow." Rosanna has still not finished her single whisky. She motions for me to join her at the kitchen island. I pour myself a scotch on the rocks.

"Who says fortune favours the brave? Fortune favours the stubborn." I whisper to no one.

"No Rowan, fortune favours the resilient." She shouts back to humiliate my whisper.

"I'll drink to that; you are definitely resilient," I say with respect and humility.

Chapter Eight: Convincing a Council

05:45 am is a lie in these days. Rosanna has been banging on the door for a good few minutes before I manage to fumble my way to the lock and mumble a greeting to her. She has dressed down for today, jeans and a T-shirt. She often makes a point of not paying respect to the council by dressing to not impress. I let her have the room and I get dressed in the bathroom, sadly my conscience compels me to wear a suit. When I return Rosanna has laid out a selection of documents to sign and a pile of statistics for this morning's debate. She throws me a pen and I sign a variety of pre-written letters thanking citizens for their support, many are relieved I am still alive and kicking.

Yesterday has served as a reminder that I need to make change happen as soon as possible. I could be challenged and killed at any moment. The nightmares last night had a common theme: shooting a young man. I am grateful to God that I didn't pull the trigger myself. Rosanna seems to have slept peacefully, unphased by events she apparently believes are merely 'political.'

"Where is Callum?" I asked obliviously, I am now sat with my morning coffee surveying the rest of the day in my mind.

"Don't know. Have you seen the unemployment statistics?" Rosanna doesn't look up from the paperwork on the coffee table.

"In our favour or not?"

"Depends on how you decide to present it. Fifteen hundred new applications in Scarborough for disability support and seven hundred and forty in Richmond. Other areas were less dramatic, two hundred and seventy-four in Harrogate and only eight hundred and sixty-one in Skipton. We expected Skipton to be much worse."

"Rosanna, how can I present those statistics in a positive light?" I ask with blatant desperation.

"Look at the demographics here. Harrogate has barely any claims, why is there such a discrepancy in mental illness? Use that! Also, these are people who clearly need support, the claims that people were leaving their jobs for a benefit cheque has been wildly over-exaggerated."

"I think you were right last night. Talk about the long term, that's a stronger argument."

We arrive at Castle Howard for 7:30 am. As we walk through the journalist's courtyard, I can't help but feel relieved that they want to talk about mental health rather than duelling. I make a conscious effort not to look at the noticeboard as we march through reception. I can already hear the bustle of activity in the chess hall, half of those who enter will never return home. We walk up the central staircase and find our way to the meeting room on the second floor.

The North Yorkshire county council has grasped the Geniocracy system with both hands. Instead of titles like *treasurer* and *home secretary* that they used to have in England, we have been given titles based on chess pieces. I am *Black Square Rook* which essentially means the minister of intra-county affairs. Esther is the *King* (Treasurer), and Katherine is *Queen* (First Minister). Esther is already in her seat, buried in sheets plastered with numbers. She is hoping to use those numbers to bury me instead.

There are eight councillors based on the eight power pieces in chess. Currently, six women and two men although that could change at any given moment in our system. Each councillor has a member of staff who is allowed to attend meetings, their *pawn*. Rosanna is my *pawn* and Callum is officially her assistant but unofficially my second *pawn*. I take my seat, like a true rook, on the fringe of the table. The next to arrive is Anthony, the *White Square Rook*, my incompetent counterpart. He is meant to be responsible for inter-county affairs, but he is only responsible for his own interests. He nods to me and takes his seat, he completely ignores Rosanna behind me, much to her amusement.

The remaining councillors file in, most of them deep in discussion with their *pawns*. Katherine is last to arrive, she looks like she hasn't slept much, collapsing into her chair at the head of the table. She glares at us all and like school children we hush each other until it falls silent. Rosanna enjoys the hushing far too much and is told to shut up by Matthew, Clare's *pawn*. This only makes Rosanna hush even louder until Katherine herself intervenes by clearing her throat.

Katherine Tyne has been our First Minister for twelve years. She is short in stature but not short in determination. After winning her seat on the council she challenged the then First Minister, Councilor Glades, within a week of taking her seat. She is truly no-nonsense and has only seen fifteen challenges in her twelve years, that is a marker of respect. She personally executed all fifteen.

As she ties her hair back, she speaks matter-of-factly, "I have been up all night dealing with some idiots firing fireworks into West Yorkshire on the border. I am not in the mood for a long debate. I want succinct arguments and an agreement on policy by the end of this meeting. Agreed?" We all nod in agreement, except Rosanna who just resentfully stares at Matthew. "Councilor Schofield, the floor is yours." My heart rate elevates a little.

"I was thinking it would be good to hear from you all before I make my statement. Just to assess the mood of the council. Let's start with Anthony, what are your thoughts?" Anthony is visibly annoyed by my manipulation of the situation and shoots me a glare. He can't side with the majority if he is to speak first.

"I have heard good things from many citizens. There seems to be enthusiastic public support for the recognition of mental illness as a disability. However, the economic situation, as I have discussed with Rowan at great length, deeply concerns me. I am interested to hear what Esther has to say about the situation." I was wrong, he has managed to back no one once again and what's more, he has brought Esther into the debate sooner than I had intended.

"The economic situation is dire," Esther jumps in before I can cut Anthony off, "I am sure you have all seen the welfare recipient claims from yesterday. We cannot afford that level of support for long. We will have to divert some of the precious research funding Rowan is always banging on about to the welfare system. Alternatively, we can backtrack, which would make more sense."

"No. That would be a grave mistake. We are all sat here mentally healthy, as far as I know, and that is a privilege we all take for granted. When we discussed implementing this legislation, we all recognised that there would be short term economic distractions. Yes, there have been a fair few welfare claims, however, they are only claiming. Many of those citizens will not qualify for support as their GPs have not diagnosed them as severely unwell. They will return to work. Furthermore, if most of those people who have made claims are legitimately unwell, think of how many people we can help with a major scientific breakthrough. It is no wonder so many days work are lost to mental illness looking at the scale of the problem we have been presented with."

"So, you are pinning your hopes on an imminent scientific breakthrough?" Katherine rarely speaks in these meetings but when she does it's generally a positive indicator.

"I am not pinning my hopes on anything. There are moral reasons to continue with the trajectory we are on. But as it so happens, I have assurances from Professor Odoi that he is on the verge of a breakthrough." The room descends into murmurs of approval. Rosanna uses the moment to stick her tongue out at Matthew and Claire.

"How many weeks away?" Katherine remains composed throughout this interruption and was unimpressed by Rosanna's immature behaviour.

"It doesn't make a difference to the economic situation." Esther pleads with Katherine.

Katherine ignores her. "How many weeks away?"

"I cannot say for certain. All I have is an assurance, but I hold Professor Odoi in very high esteem. He has achieved many great things in the past. He is one of North Yorkshires greatest treasures."

"You are becoming more statesmanlike by the minute Schofield." Katherine shows a glimmer of a smile. "How about we fund this disability legislation and its associated complications for an agreed-upon amount of time. That will secure a significant amount of funding for Professor Odoi and his team and weigh leigh some of poor Esther's concerns. It will also provide us with a better estimate of how many citizens require mental health support funding."

"I see the *Queen of compromise* is with us this morning." Claire sighs sarcastically and is jeered on my Esther. "It's a shame Rowan's team have so many problems with compromise."

"Excuse me?" Rosanna has gone from basking in glory to simmering with rage in a matter of seconds.

"Well, apparently you haven't looked at the duels scheduled for this weekend. It seems your puppy Callum has been challenged to death. I see he cannot compromise and can only assume he has inherited that from his master and mistress."

I swivel in my chair and look at Rosanna. She is completely astonished. I have never seen her so confused; this is an event neither of us could have predicted.

"Before we get off track, let's vote. All in favour of a temporary continuation with limited financial support raise your hand." Katherine's vote counts as two votes which means we sail past the majority needed with seven votes to two. Claire and Esther opposed. Anthony raises his hand last, little weasel.

Rosanna and I leave in a hurry, I drop my pen on the floor in the process but can't be bothered to pick it up. Who on earth would challenge harmless Callum? We jog down the stairs to the noticeboard, papers are falling out of my bag all the way down the staircase. To our horror, the Saturday evening schedule has a table with the name *Paul Stevens* written across from *Callum Stevens.* He has been challenged by his husband.

Chapter Nine: Callum and Paul

The chauffeur brings the car around and we exit as fast as we can. The press are being entertained by Esther and Claire's rants on the steps outside about 'poor economic planning' from the council. I could not care less and do not stop when asked for a comment. As the doors of the black Range Rover close, I wonder whether we are no longer sat in a government officials' car but in the hearse driving my friend's body to his funeral.

Rosanna is in a state. She is frantically scrolling through her emails. She stops and unblinkingly reads out a message.

Hi Rosanna,

Had some stomach problems in the night. Will need a few days off to recover, don't want to give you guys anything nasty! If there is anything you need my input on just send me an email and I'll get back to you ASAP.

Cal

She is livid. "How dare he lie to me! This is our job; you literally play chess for your life. Of all the people in the world to turn to, he should have turned to us. He should have at least told us the real reason he isn't here." She starts kicking the driver's chair in front of her until he says "ow," and then she apologises profusely.

We direct the driver to a small cluster of houses in Knaresborough. Callum and Paul live in a tight-knit village, the kind of village where any drama is talked about for years on end. Callum's news will have fed the gossip monster for decades, never mind years. Rosanna marches up the driveway with a pace and vigour I cannot match. She hammers the door like a nail into a coffin.

A bedraggled Callum peers out of the window and looks ashamed. He is dressed in a woolly grey dressing gown and has a small amount of stubble which I am not used to seeing on him. He even opens the door in a manner which makes me pity him. Rosanna is having none of it and barges the door open and storms into the living room. She plonks herself down on the couch and taps her foot until we both join her on the adjacent sofa. Callum obviously feels unsettled next to me and makes a poor excuse to take a seat on an armchair positioned near the door.

"How did you find out?" Callum asked sheepishly. He isn't making eye contact with either of us.

"Oh, so you have already given up on pretending you are unwell?" Rosanna replies with venom.

"I didn't want to burden you guys last night or this morning, I know you had an important meeting." Callum's statement was sincere but unconvincing.

"Yeah, well you not telling us about your personal problems meant we were unprepared for an onslaught from Claire and Esther." Rosanna had evolved from a python into a spitting cobra.

"Calm down Rosanna, the meeting went fine. It was an awful shock, that's all. Tell us what happened. We are all ears." Callum is relieved by my intervention. Callum is not striking in appearance. He has green eyes like mine but has much darker hair. More of a brunette tinge to his blondness, I was nicknames angel in my family for my hair colour.

"Two nights ago, Paul mentioned that we hadn't had a date night in a while, and it was important that we spent time together. I agreed. He said I often back out of date nights because of work commitments and so he wanted me to guarantee that I would be there. I promised."

"He organised a babysitter yesterday morning before I left for work. Then that challenge came into the Octagon and I immediately messaged Paul to tell him what was going on and said it was going to be a stressful day. I suggested we might need to rearrange, just in case. He replied saying to message him a bit later when I had a better idea of what the day entailed and when I would be done."

"I told him what time we had agreed to conduct the challenge, but he didn't reply. He watched it online. On the way back to the Octagon he told me to come home, he hadn't cancelled the babysitter, he said. I told him I just had to drop some things off, but he didn't reply to that either."

"Upon arrival, I found this house as empty as it stands now. With one exception, there was a candle lit on the dining room table and behind it sat my miserable husband." Callum's voice broke at this point. "I asked him where the kids were, and he said one of our friends had agreed to take them for the night. When he wouldn't tell me which friend I realised what was coming." Callum had been holding it together up to this point but with that last word the man disintegrated in front of our very eyes. I moved over to him and sat on the arm of the armchair. I put my arm around him and shook him gently.

"Keep going." I encourage.

"He listed off hundreds of little fights we have had. He talked about how I was always working. Apparently, I take my marriage to my job more seriously than my marriage to my husband. He said I was an incompetent father because I was never around when they were younger and now I don't know how to interact with them. I disagreed but he couldn't be reasoned with. We became quiet for a long time, hours, and then he broke the silence by mentioning a divorce lawyer. I couldn't take it and started shouting things I now regret."

"His lawyer had advised him to file for a divorce. However, with my prominent position in government, the lawyer thought I would win a custody battle for Jamie and Ewan. So, he advised Paul to challenge me to the death. The lawyer said that was Paul's only real option!"

"I debated fiercely, Rowan you would have been impressed if you had heard me, I explained challenging me was not his only option. He could stay with me. We could wait out this rough patch. We could live to fight another day, together." The passion in Callum's voice exploded as he said this. "We could learn to love each other once more."

"He wasn't persuaded," I said this with the softest voice I could muster but the statement alone filled the room with dread, and I regretted saying it immediately. Rosanna was up on her feet throwing a small rock she had found somewhere between her hands. She likes to fiddle with things while she thinks.

"The challenge is to the death but all you actually want is custody rights?" asked Rosanna.

"No Rosanna! It is years of built-up resentment. This man truly hates me. He wants to kill me within the law, and custody is his excuse to do so."

"But you are still in love with him?" I ask.

"With all of my heart."

"Then you will not be able to play to the death! This is a disagreement which should be settled by lawyers, not by chess." Rosanna was addressing this to me rather than Callum, but Callum replied anyway.

"This is a problem which I should have foreseen. Whatever happens, my children stay with me."

Rosanna sat down with her head in her hands. Through a prison window of fingers, I heard the words. Truly horrible words. "You will lose."

Callum was indignant. "Get out. I will win, just you watch."

We leave in silence. Callum doesn't say or do anything else except lock the door of his empty house behind us. I get into the passenger seat and allow Rosanna to have the back seats all to herself. She lays face down across the three seats making a disturbing angry groaning noise. I leave her to it and for once I look at my own emails.

Chapter Ten: A Crime of Passion

Saturday has come around without a word from Callum. Tensions in the Octagon have been tense, not only because of Callum's situation but because the voluntary unemployment statistics are continuing to rise with limited reprise for compliments from people with mental illnesses. The situation is also worsening by the day in other aspects. Companies are complaining about the additional bureaucracy involved with making the work environment safe for people with undisclosed mental illnesses.

Businesses anonymously claimed the additional costs are making them less likely to employ someone with a mental illness and citizens are saying we have worsened that situation as defining mental illness as a disability meant people have to declare that on job applications, increasing the potential for discrimination.

I am seething with anger. I sit on the edge of my bed and cry. I cry not for my sake, nor for the sake of those with severe mental illness. I cry because I realise what life has been like for people with disabilities ever since the term was invented. Have we politicians helped? Has the disability label allowed political correctness to reign whilst pain and suffering continue under a mist of pity? Am I part of a system which is causing pain to those who have suffered more than I could ever imagine? I console myself with notions that appreciation of the disability label is protective against the historical abuse.

I cry because I feel helpless. I think of all that I have lost just to get mental health defined as a disability and even that hasn't necessarily helped my citizens. I realise I had selfish intentions, I wanted to light a flame that sparked a revolution for my legacy's sake. I had selfish intentions but at least I was trying to do good. Imagine a teenage boy takes a girl on a date for the first time. As they are walking home the girl mentions she is cold, and the boy gives her his jacket. Now, the boy who gave her his jacket did so because he wanted to have a second date, or he wanted a girlfriend, or he wanted a kiss. However, whatever his intentions, the girl has got a jacket and feels warmer. Good has been done. Does it matter what the intentions were?

Yes is the answer but the question doesn't really apply to my situation. I am hypothesising to escape my own conscience. My good deed is debatable with these new statistics haunting my nightmares. Nevertheless, intentions do matter. I want North Yorkshire to rise from the ashes because my people are in bondage. That motive at least, is pure.

I get up and have breakfast. Rosanna has spent the night on the couch. Her workload is unmanageable without Callum, but I can't hire a replacement yet. He could survive tonight. It's unlikely, but he could. I get to back to the barrage of bad news.

At 7:30 pm we set off for Castle Howard. Neither of us has eaten, neither of us has heard from Callum and neither of us is sober. However, this is not a party; we are both intoxicated to stop us from vomiting with nerves. When I was challenged I didn't feel nervous, I was in charge of my own destiny. When your friend is challenged there is nothing you can do, and that is much worse. When we arrive I vomit anyway, thankfully the journalists aren't allowed near the chauffeur drop-off point.

When we arrive in the courtyard there is no one there. It is the first time I have appreciated the astounding beauty of Castle Howard. For some reason, every busy place is nicer when you are the only one there. We walk through to the chess hall

75

and its appearance has changed dramatically. There is only one cameraman who looks like a student on his first shift after qualifying. He haphazardly moves the camera around the tables, unsure of which duel to focus on. This must be terrible viewing.

The chess hall has high ceilings, Victorian style, with a series of modern paintings positioned in the wallpaper. These were inserted after the revolution and depict famous battle from the wars of independence in 2085. All the duelling tables are dark wood, making the hall quite threatening.

Generally, weekend duels are a thing of the past. They are outside normal working hours. The only people challenging on weekends are jilted lovers and unhappy marriages. Speaking of unhappy marriages, I see Callum, sat alone, on the table looking at his pawns in a daze. He does not look like a man confident of surviving the night. I read that in the middle ages the great warriors duelled with swords, I imagine they looked confident before the battle. Now great thinkers duel with chess pieces and look unwell beforehand.

Fortunately, most of the tables around Callum are empty and so Rosanna and I take a seat nearby. The inexperienced cameraman thinks he is in luck. Rosanna and I look like we are about to duel which attracts his attention. It's not until Rosanna laughs in his face that he turns the camera away from us to an actual duel on the other side of the room. Callum looks at us and we see the remnant of a drying tear on his cheek.

"Thank you for coming guys. I knew you would come. I am sorry for how I reacted the other night. If this is to be my last night, I want you to know: It has been the greatest honour of my life to have worked with you because we have done great things for so many people. I know your work will continue my legacy." He said this like he had been up all night preparing it while he tossed and turned. It was said with emotion, but the emotion was dulled by extreme tiredness.

I outstretch my arm to dissuade Rosanna from blurting out something she would regret. She scowls at me.

"Callum, if that is truly how you feel, then you know you should stay with us. We need you alive to continue all the work we have done." I plead with him. That's putting it nicely. I beg him.

"It has been an honour working with you, but my children are my life. There is no life worth living without them." Evidently, he had anticipated our response to his previous monologue as this statement also felt preprepared.

Just as Rosanna's anger is about to break through the social wall I have enclosed her in with my outstretched arm, Paul arrives. He also looks shattered but in his eyes, it is clear he has come here with steely determination. He wants to win. Callum wants him back in his life. They say nothing to each other. Paul looks intently at the board. Callum looks intently at Paul.

The most bored official I have ever seen come over and starts the chess clocks. As the challenger, Paul is given black. Callum opens with a bog-standard Queen's gambit. Rosanna is watching with her head in her hands. In a flash, Paul replies with his knight and the game is off. With each turn, Callum takes longer and longer to play, often appearing to forget it is his turn and gazing at Paul instead. I can feel his love for Paul emanating across the room to me, but Paul is unmoved. Steadfast in his decision. In fifteen minutes, the game is on its last legs. Callum is impeded by a pawn wall of his own making, no power pieces left. Paul is causing mayhem with two rooks. The tears are free flowing on both sides now, Paul is not emotionless anymore.

Rosanna leaves the room; all her limbs were shaking, and she kept running her hands through her hair and breathing heavily. As I turned to make sure she was ok I saw Katherine looking on from the edge of the room. She nods to me. I nod back. No words are needed.

Paul is one move away from checkmate when Callum finally breaks the silence.

"Paul." He says but this name falls upon deaf ears. "Can I just say something to Rosanna before you kill me, a dying declaration?" Paul sits back, checks the clock to make sure he has enough time, and nods. I jump up and rush to the women's bathroom to get Rosanna. She is washing her face when I fling the door open and shout, "Callum wants to speak to you before he loses."

We rush back. There was no point washing her face, her cheeks are clad with tears once more. When we arrive back in the chess hall Callum is looking at a photo in his wallet. He is a wreck of a man. Even the cameraman is making an effort to avoid their table, no one wants to see this. Rosanna kneels by his side and he whispers in her ear. She does not respond. She remains knelt on the floor whilst Paul makes his last move.

I am tapped on the shoulder and turn to see Katherine. I had kept it together up until then, I burst into tears and she holds me. The cameraman turns to capture this on film, but I couldn't care less what the world sees. Katherine whispers, "Trust me, look away." She holds me. She holds me whilst the official walks over to the table and places the gun down. She holds me as I hear Callum's sobs. She holds me when the security personnel drag him out through the hallowed walls. She lets me go only for Rosanna to take over. We are holding each other when the gunshot rings out from the executioner's office across the courtyard.

When we eventually get ourselves together we turn to see the hall empty. As we walk out, propping each other up like pensioners trying to cross the road, Katherine is sat outside.

"Come for a drink. I'm buying," she says.

Chapter Eleven: Conversations with Katherine

Castle Howard is the official government building of North Yorkshire, and it has living quarters in the east wing reserved for the first minister. Very few people enter the private section as all government business is conducted in the meeting rooms on the first floor. Katherine leads us through a maze of corridors and through *Private* signs until we enter what feels like a flat in Leeds it is so far away.

The mood is sombre, to say the least. No one has spoken but there is a mutual understanding amongst the three of us. What has just happened is the worst aspect of our political system. Autocracy was oppressive, communist and fascist ideologies made democracy farcical and now Geniocracy is excusing murder. Is there any hope for politics?

We sit around Katherine's kitchen bench and all stare at our drinks. Katherine looks crestfallen. I am temporarily distracted from my sorrow by wondering why this event has affected Katherine so deeply. She did imply she has been in a similar situation before. She opens by saying, "In my many years as First Minister I have learnt that when something important needs to be said, there is no such thing as a right time or right place. Nevertheless, I have never had to say something so important at quite as bad a time as this."

"Are we here to be berated? If so, I am not in the mood." Rosanna's usual flare had dissipated. She sounded helpless and is already getting ready to leave.

"No, I have asked you here to give you a warning. I know it's been a rough day, but the weeks and months ahead will not be any easier. This is one of the few opportunities I have to speak to you before things get out of hand." Katherine says this without diverting her gaze from her drink. I am not in the mood for hyperbole, but I am still intrigued.

"Look Katherine, I know the mental health legislation is on shaky ground but discussing the failure of that after my friend's death is completely out of order," I say this with more aggression than I intend and quickly remember she is my boss. "I am so sorry, please excuse my outburst. I am not myself." I say quickly.

This apology was unnecessary, Katherine completely understands and couldn't care less about my anger. She waves her hands and says, "No, no! Don't worry. I should have been clearer. I am facing imminent danger and the implications will affect you in the long term."

Rosanna and I look at each other. Katherine has been a staple of life in North Yorkshire for twelve years. She regularly appears on television as carefree and intellectually undefeatable. This perception had only been strengthened by my observations during what feels like thousands of council meetings. To hear her talking like this is a grave concern and takes us by surprise.

"As you know, once a month the four First Ministers convene to discuss national matters. I am usually shunned, being North Yorkshire and all." I couldn't believe my ears, Katherine shunned! "The county of North Yorkshire is treated as the back garden of West Yorkshire. Moreover, any 50:50 split on a decision is decided in favour of whichever side West Yorkshire takes. It is incredibly frustrating, but I feel I have achieved many things for this county, nonetheless." We both nod to indicate our respect for her achievements.

"For the last two years, West Yorkshire have been trying to change the *challenge eligibility criteria*. I know it sounds boring, but it is extremely important. You are aware of course, that to challenge a member of a county council you have to be born in that county or have lived there for ten years. West Yorkshire claims that in order to maximise our potential we need free movement of politics across the borders. For example, a great North Yorkshire businesswoman sets up a business in East Yorkshire. She is unhappy with the legislation in East Yorkshire and wishes to challenge a councillor to make some changes to business law. However, she is prevented from doing so because she is a North Yorkshire citizen. So, she decides to live there for ten years under terrible business restrictions until she is eligible to challenge. West Yorkshire sees that as ten years of lost progress. It annoys me that they used an example of a North Yorkshire businesswoman as if that would win me over."

"I can see their point!" I interject.

"No. You don't." This is the first time she has looked away from her whisky. "The West Yorkshire commission have always wanted a united Yorkshire political system. This would mean 36 council posts based in one city, representing the whole country. No individual county councils. Only one first minister. To execute such a change would need the consent of all four counties."

"Ok?"

"They do not have a consensus yet. Not even a
second vote, yet. So, I put it to you, Rowan
Schofield, what would you do in their position? If
you really are the person destined to liberate North
Yorkshire as councillor Stewart once suggested
you were, show me how well you understand this
game we call politics!"

In my mind, a chessboard appears. West
Yorkshire vs The Others. Political systems and
policies move in my mind like pieces being taken
by each other, policies being nullified of their
potential to cause the change West Yorkshire so
desire. We sit in silence as I make my theoretical
moves. But the game is too finely balanced. There
is no way for West Yorkshire to win this debate
with the current system in practice.

"Don't you see Rowan!" Rosanna appeared
emboldened by being treated like a council
member in Katherine Tyne's presence. "Not
everything is like a game of chess. When the
game doesn't work for you, change the game."

"What?" I ask haphazardly whilst still
contemplating the original enigma proposed to me.

"If they remove the citizenship requirement to challenge officials on a local council, they can challenge all the first ministers individually with West Yorkshire citizens. They would be able to create the united Yorkshire political system without to reach a consensus with the existing First Ministers."

"That's assuming they are better than our chess players." I retort with a patriotic air of defiance.

"Keep going, Rosanna." Katherine encourages against my will. Rosanna is making me look like a fool and I resent her a little bit for it.

"The cards are already decked in their favour. The other counties are playing without their queens. Who is it who verifies that all children are given the same level of chess education? The councils do. What if West Yorkshire council are not upholding their end of the bargain. What if their students are taught more? Furthermore, what if an accomplished chess player, a member of West Yorkshire's county council per se, decided they didn't want to settle for a lowly councillor position in West Yorkshire when they could be First Minister of North Yorkshire. The challenges would be never-ending."

"Bingo," says Katherine, who is depressed at her own understanding of the situation.

The last time I had heard that word it came from my long-time friend Councillor Stewart. Not only am I failing to improve North Yorkshire's position in Yorkshire as he beseeched me to do, but we are also apparently on the brink of a complete collapse into West Yorkshire's hands.

"These are wild conspiracy theories," I say complacently but really I am panicking and annoyed that I didn't think of the answer Katherine was looking for before Rosanna. I reprimand myself in my mind for being so jealous and conceited.

"Conspiracy theory or not, we will know soon enough. The council voted on a small change to the *challenge eligibility criteria* last night. West Yorkshire got their second vote in the East. You are now able to challenge after five years of residence. It won't be long until we are inundated with challenges."

Rosanna and I are gobsmacked. I feel like a child in a science lesson who had just been taught about the anatomy of the heart but now I am dissecting a heart in my very hands. Our theory was about to be put to the test.

87

"It comes into force next week." Katherine finished.

In the darkness on the drive home, I think of Callum. Rosanna is sat on the opposite side of the car watching the raindrops chase each other down the window. We never get a moments peace in this job.

Chapter Twelve: Making Appearances

The worst part of being a politician is making public appearance at places you are obligated to be. No scrap that. The worst part of being a politician is making speeches at public appearances where you are obligated to be, but you would rather not. I am sat on the banks of the Skipton canal about to take a canal boat ride with a series of businessmen and women. The sky reflects my mood, dour.

The boat arrives at my stop and I walk down the muddied steps to climb aboard. I am greeted by a wave of sickening "Hellos" and "Aaays." Within seconds I am accosted by the representative from Taylor's tea. He firmly grasps my shoulder with one gigantic hand and vigorously shakes my hand with the other hand. "Thank you for joining us today! You are a personal hero of mine and of the Taylor's corporation, we have every faith that you will restore North Yorkshire to the economic hub that it once was for us."

I grapple in my mind for his name. "I am so relieved to hear you say that! I have heard rumours that with East Yorkshire's acquisition of York they have been trying to tempt you away from us."

"Haha, cutting to the chase! Just like I would expect from a politician of your calibre. Determined not to waste precious breath." His smiles and laughing make me feel queasy. "It is true, we have received numerous offers to have lunch with East Yorkshire representatives and even an invitation to look at a discounted warehouse that they would offer us. However, your mental health legislation persuaded Sierra Cole to stay put."

"Well, Sierra Cole is the first CEO I have heard praise the legislation. Please enlighten me as to how the legislation benefits Taylor's Tea?" I inquire politely but be under no illusions I am absolutely desperate for the answer. Anything I can use in a future press conference.

"It doesn't help us in the slightest. In fact, it has increased our administration costs and we have lost several key workers to the unemployment roll. However, for a company our size, we have not lost as many as we could have done. Mrs Cole was pleased as this implies the working conditions at Taylor's are excellent."

90

"Well, I have always known Taylor's was a good place to work. However, increased costs sound like a negative to me." I further my inquest.

"Quite correct! We have had to change some of our policies and procedures to adjust the finances. The reason Mrs Cole could not be tempted was that she saw something in you. It has been a long time since a politician has attempted something so daring and controversial in North Yorkshire. We have had a lot of sheep on our council. She is confident that with you in charge one day, business in North Yorkshire will flourish."

This is not a compliment. He is trying to establish my intentions to report back to his boss. If I were to deny any aspirations of leadership, would that dissuade Sierra from staying in the North?

"Please tell Mrs Cole how honoured I am to have received such high praise from a CEO as accomplished as herself. I have aspirations for some significant reform to business structure in the near future, I am sure I can create some more opportunities for Taylor's."

He seems pleased with my response and let me past to enter the cabin and get myself a drink. There is no rest for the wicked. I notice a Coca-Cola administrator eyeing me from across the cabin. I make a deliberate point of pouring myself a Coke, taking a sip and exaggerating my enjoyment of the drink by as much as I can muster. She correctly interprets this as an invitation. I pretend not to have noticed her.

"Hello, our knight in shining armour!" Her smile is as broad as a Cheshire cat's. "We would like to take this opportunity to convey our thanks, our institutional costs are much lower than they were in the West." She is one of those corporate machines who never says 'I' or 'me' it's always 'we' or 'us' like she is literally the company in human form. "We would like to ask, however, about the long-term plans for the mental health legislation. What are your plans for the future?"

It is going to be a long afternoon.

By dinner time I have spoken to over twenty representatives and drunk so much coke I have been basically living in the toilet, that is until I had to switch to water when Harrogate Spa water asked me if I didn't like their water. The afternoon is a long way from over. I still have a speech to make. Dinner is short and I stand on the edge of the boat to speak. No microphones, no lectern, no notes.

"Ladies and Gentlemen. I have spoken to a lot of people on this surprisingly large canal boat..." a small polite chuckle ripples through the audience. "but I am sure I have missed some people and for that, I sincerely apologise. I have drunk so many free drinks provided by our great North Yorkshire firms that I fear I have spent more time in the toilet than speaking with people I need to speak with." A real laugh now emerges from the crowded boat.

"I have noticed a common trend. It seems to me, and correct me if I am wrong, that many of you are pleased with the newfound confidence of the local government but are concerned about the additional costs imposed on you by some recent legislature reform." Nods of agreement from all the companies reassure me of their attention.

"I realise that the short term has been difficult, but I want to inspire hope in you all. There is a light at the end of the tunnel. I hope if anything has become clear, the scale of the problem of mental illness has been highlighted to you all from recent weeks. I must admit, more people were unwell than even I had anticipated. This is sad news for business, but it is worse for those individuals who live with minimal hope and in relentless pain. We are confident of a pharmacological breakthrough. We believe we are on the cusp of developing a drug which will reduce the suffering of these people and nullify the impact of mental health illnesses on your companies. Imagine, no sick days for stress, no workers with depression or anxiety. Imagine the impact on your staff. I appreciate these words are only that, words. So, give us time, and when we deliver, remember what we promised here today."

This short speech is greeted with rapturous applause but that in itself is meaningless, these are professional people pleasers, what matters is what they tell their bosses. I leave the boat at the next stop and breathe a sigh of relief. Finally, I can return to doing important things.

Chapter Thirteen: Following the News

When I arrive home, Rosanna is sat wrapped in a blanket, knees up and staring with absolute horror at the Television. At the sound of the door opening, without looking at me, she says, "Katherine was right, it has begun."

I plant myself on the sofa next to her and try to grasp what is happening without asking stupid questions. It seems that whenever I want to hear the headlines, the news is showing some feature piece instead. I am growing more and more frustrated until eventually, it cuts back to Amanda Buckle.

Our top stories this evening: Katherine Tyne has been formerly challenged by cabinet rival Esther Somerville. In a statement released this afternoon Miss Somerville denounced the First Minister as 'spineless' and "obstructing the collective mission to improve life across Yorkshire as a whole."

Neither of us say anything. We just sit in silence and contemplate what this means for us.

Councillor vs Councillor duels are huge events. However, we need Katherine in power. Esther will disband the mental health reform within seconds of gaining control of the council. Esther is an ardent supporter of a United Yorkshire. For us, Esther Somerville spells severe trouble.

"Have we caused this?" I ask Rosanna betraying shame and fear in my voice.

"I was worried about that too, so I asked around. I spoke with that idiot pawn Matthew, Claire's understudy, he was trying to be smug with me but let it slip that Esther has recently had some significant backing from the West. When I say significant, I mean financial incentives that you would not believe."

"How much are we talking? Could we afford to pay her off, get her to stop?"

"Six figures."

"Well, that answers that question."

Once again silence descends, and my thoughts turn grey. Katherine is yet to make a statement to the public. This is not unusual for her; she only makes comments about challenges once she has defeated the opponent. Obviously, I have every confidence that she will defeat Esther. Every confidence. No doubts at all…

"We should make a statement." Rosanna interrupts my spiralling.

"No, we should hire a replacement for Callum." I say distract both of us.

Technically I am not supposed to have a second pawn. To get around this we provide the job title as an assistant to the pawn. It is a bit of a joke, but so is a lot of bureaucracy. It is a very competitive position, nonetheless. Many members of the public like to have experience in politics, especially if they are planning on a future political career for themselves. That is not the type of person we want to employ. We want someone committed to our cause, someone with a fierce sense of loyalty but capable in their own right. It is not uncommon for councillors to be challenged by pawns or administrative staff. Hiring a loyal candidate will hopefully reduce the risk of being challenged by a former advisor.

We interview in Castle Howard. It is an ingenious interview tactic from Rosanna. Applicants will show their true colours here, those obsessed with power will struggle to contain themselves when in the political hub of North Yorkshire. They will show their wild aspirations of being top dog in the subtle things they say and do. The applicants we are interested in will be unimpressed if not slightly bored by the surroundings, they will be more interested in us.

We have also deliberately left it to short notice to announce our interview slots. Although I am not convinced by this approach, Callum had always sworn by it. The less time they have to prepare, the more likely to get a true impression of their character. We also want employees who are quick on their feet, it isn't possible to be prepared for everything in this line of work.

Finally, Rosanna's last trick, and by far her favourite is to pretend to be the receptionist and see how the candidates interact with her when they see her as a secretary. She also thinks those who have done their homework will know who she is and not be fooled by the receptionist gambit. They are going to work for her after all, so I will let her interview however she wants. I take my seat behind a mahogany desk and await the interviewees.

The first chap looks significantly older than me. He is a classic silver fox, grey hair but devilishly handsome. As he enters the room, Rosanna gives me a shake of the head. Not him apparently. He is polite enough and definitely bright, but it becomes apparent that this man has aspirations for office himself and would be a danger for us. Rosanna was right about this one.

The afternoon continues in this vein. Applicant after applicant getting the shake of the head from Rosanna as she opens the door for them enter the room. She has set up a little receptionist office in the corridor and surveys the candidates from the moment they arrive in the waiting room. It is not until the dying embers of the day that I finally get a nod. In relief, I straighten up in my chair and realign my suit. I feel like I am being interviewed! A small woman enters the room with an amazing kind smile on her face.

"Counsellor Schofield, what an honour." She beams, she remains standing behind the chair.

"The honour is all mine, please, take a seat." I reply and she promptly sits down. She is sat bolt upright and looks incredibly smart. "Tell me a little bit about yourself."

The intriguing lady takes a deep breath and leans back. "I am a woman of few words so I will simply say this. My name is Hannah Reed. I am a North Yorkshire 3rd Battalion Veteran and served in York during the border wars to keep the peace. I admire what you are doing, I want to continue to serve my county and I believe the best way for me to do so is at your side. Or should I say the side of your pretend receptionist."

She can see by my reaction that I am impressed with her condensed resumé. She responds by repositioning herself on her chair. "I probably shouldn't have said that I recognised Rosanna, that was a card in my favour." She says with incredible honesty. I understand why Rosanna likes her. We are looking for loyal, who is more loyal that a soldier. We are also looking to start a revolution, who better than a warrior.

"You're hired." I announce.

"Don't you have to discuss all the applicants with Rosanna?" She is astounded with my declaration but regains her composure quickly.

"I know she already wants you. Come to the Octagon at 6:45am and I will do your induction and contracts and things. Is that ok?"

"6:45am! That's a lie in!" She stands as she says this, winks and shakes my hand. As she leaves I feel hopeful for the future for the first time in months. Things are beginning to piece themselves together for our cause. Rosanna enters the room and jumps around with glee.

"She is perfect! Just what we need." She says whilst bouncing around the room as if the floor is a trampoline.

"I completely agree! She has literally made my day brighter!"

I sour the mood quickly by turning the TV on in the room and switching to the chess channel. Rosanna stops jumping as she sees Katherine Tyne appear on the screen and she is transfixed by the board.

"Katherine's going to win." She correctly interprets from the board.

"You're getting better at chess if you can tell that!" She seems pleased with my compliment and I am pleased with the board. Esther is struggling on her King's side and looks visibly nervous. Katherine turns to the camera and smiles. At this point I know it's all over for Esther. I switch it off. Rosanna and I smile at each other and start collecting our things from the room. Business is done for the day. As I turn the light out my phone receives a notification.

Breaking News: Esther Somerville defeated and executed. Read our analysis including predictions for next King piece of North Yorkshire.

I close the door quietly behind me.

Chapter Fourteen: Reshuffle

When a councillor challenges another councillor, it causes two problems. The first is that a cabinet position is left unfilled. To allow a new councillor to join us around the table a chess tournament is arranged with the winner installed at the pleasure of the first minister. The second problem interests me more. When a councillor is killed, a more senior position becomes available for the vultures to swoop in on. King's piece, or treasurer, would be a huge advantage for me. If I was in control of the economy I could weigh leigh concerns about the mental health unemployment numbers. I could manipulate the research funding in my favour. It is the solution to all my problems.

Following Katherine's recent disclosure of confidence in me I feel like I have a good opportunity to be the first to feast on the carcass. I tell Rosanna to go back ahead of me and prepare the paperwork for Ms Reed's appointment. She understands and leaves with a nod and a thumbs up. I sit on the sofa where young Malenkovic had sat a few weeks ago. I feel like a challenger here, desperate to gain more power, fidgeting in my seat and conscious of mild sweating.

It is about 10 minutes before Katherine appears in the entrance hall. The receptionist had informed me that Katherine had taken a walk after the execution. A gale has been blowing through the courtyard and Katherine looks windswept as a result. She stops just inside the door and drops her umbrella on the floor. The next minute is spent removing loose strands of hair from her face and checking the contents of her bag for any water damage.

Once she has sorted her appearance she strides with confidence through the hallway. As she catches a glimpse of me she giggles to herself and says sarcastically, "Who'd have thought you would be here at this time?"

"I think *coincidence* may not ring true in this circumstance." I say with a smirk. She beckons for me to follow her and once again I find myself in Katherine's kitchen, whisky in hand and sitting in silence.

"So, Mr Schofield, or should I say *Black Square Rook* how can I *promote*, sorry, help you today." She is struggling to hold back laughter. I think this is probably a good sign, she knows my intentions and does not seem to be opposed to the idea.

"I think Esther Somerville was out of her mind to challenge you and was a terrible chancellor. You should make me *King*. I am a loyal supporter after all." The flattery managed to dull this demand and make it sound moderately more acceptable. If a journalist were in this room they would be having a field day.

"I feel like people have lost some respect for me." Katherine contemplated, "I am a very good chess player, I am a very skilled communicator but more than both of those things, I am an excellent politician." I could sense what she was about to say. "I agree you would make a valuable *King* piece; however, I have more pressing concerns. For example, with Esther Somerville dead, I would imagine Claire will shortly be receiving a visit from the West with a pay cheque in hand."

I take a huge gulp of whisky.

"So here are my conditions." She elaborates. "I will appoint you chancellor, but on one condition. Let's be honest, being chancellor will change the game for your recent legislation. You have a lot to gain, I wasn't born this morning Schofield.

Therefore, this is the condition: you challenge Claire and remove her from my council."

I finish the remaining whisky and gently place the glass on the kitchen island. Silence washes over the room.

"That would leave two empty slots on the council. What is to say that West Yorkshire will not find people to take their place given the new citizenship laws." I inquire.

"Nervous are we?" She is excruciatingly happy, "That is a valid possibility but removing Claire would kill two birds with one stone. It would truly deter future challenges to us and consolidate my trust in you."

This is not about dealing with the West Yorkshire situation. This is a power grab from the woman who is already in power. My intervention would give Katherine undivided loyalty in the council and ammunition against the West for the foreseeable future. This benefits her more than me. But I am weak, and she is strong. What would Callum recommend?

I stretch out my hand and she takes it forcefully. "We have a deal. I will give you 48 hours to challenge Councillor Claire Jones. Win and you receive the seat of chancellor. Lose and North Yorkshire is doomed."

As I exit the flat, I tie my scarf around my neck and then skip down the stairs. I feel alive. I call Rosanna mid staircase. "Rosanna, it's going to be a tough few days for us. I am on my way to challenge Claire, looks like your nemesis Matthew may be out of a job soon."

"Are you sure?" Came the muffled reply.

"Win and Katherine will make me *king*."

"Challenge her before you leave then. She won't be able to sleep tonight." Rosanna has ruthless insight into the human mind.

I hang up and quickly find myself in the executioner's office. I am greeted by a young man who is startled by the appearance of a councillor at this time of night. He shakes the mouse to reawaken his computer and then gestures for me to come forward to the desk.

"Dispatch a challenge request to Councillor Jones tonight." I say with extreme calmness which makes my statement even more shocking to the poor receptionist.

"Are you sure councillor?" He manages to pull himself together as he says this.

"Absolutely young man. Oh, and can you book us a slot at table 14, I am a big fan of that table." Table 14 would bring me some reassurance after Mr Malenkovic's performance.

"I can do that sir, I must remind you, however, that the date and time are at Councillor Jones' discretion." He has recovered his professionalism and now states this in a robotic manner.

"Table 14 is enough for me." I reply.

I enter the night on foot, wind gusts behind me scattering leaves around the courtyard like a pinball machine. I see a runner dispatch my challenge to Claire and I walk on with pride. I managed to get a position on the council without challenging a councillor, I suppose it's fair that I don't progress until I prove my credentials at chess. I receive a text from Rosanna:

Is it a go?

Chapter Fifteen: Preparing for War

This morning has been hectic. The news outlets are astounded by the news, dubbing the reports as an indication of an internal council war coming to the foreground. Newspapers have photoshopped pictures of Katherine and I wrestling Esther and Claire to the ground. Claire has gone on record at 5am this morning saying that the challenge was unprovoked and so she will have no hesitation in executing me. 5am… I guess Rosanna was right; she didn't sleep well.

Rosanna has blocked all my calls for the day and is answering all my correspondence. She has essentially barricaded me in my bedroom with a chess board. The only time she breaks this isolation is at lunchtime when she tells me that Claire has accepted the challenge for a late-night session tonight. She believes this is a good sign; claims Claire is probably having a nap so needs to play late in the evening. I take comfort in Rosanna's wild psychology, although I am not sure I believe it all.

I am sick to death of staring at this chess board. I will have to play black as I am the challenger and so I am revising my high school notes on classic openings. Rosanna has provided me with a comprehensive list of all Claire's previous matches, and it appears she consistently plays the Napoleon Attack, consistently is a stretch, she has only been challenged twice. I am sure she is currently analysing my game with Malenkovic as well, but she has even less to go on. Malenkovic was so incompetent she won't learn much from that game.

Rosanna enters with a grimace on her face. She has got changed into her duelling dress, emblazoned with the Yorkshire White Rose. Nevertheless, she looks very composed and I must admit, strikingly beautiful.

"Do you want to make a statement? Explain the challenge to the public? I think Katherine would appreciate a public denouncement of Claire to discourage future politicians with her views." Rosanna asked.

"I think that would be a good idea, Claire is painting me as an undignified aggressor and that is not the image I want to portray. Also, with the political gossip today, making Claire and Esther seem like an evil alliance will only increase the pressure on our councillor Jones."

"I have another idea, If I may…" Rosanna has that twinkle in her sea blue eyes which means she has some complicated psychological scheme in mind. "You have been studying her games today right?" I nod in agreement. "Well, why don't you make your speech on camera with her Napoleon attack on a chess board in the background. Then, when she sees it she will think you have prepared a defence for her opening and will change her mind about playing it tonight. That will put the game on your terms, make her uncomfortable before the duel has even begun." She is wearing a broad smile like that of a devious dictator.

"Aha, I like your idea. I am still going to prepare a defence though; she may see through it."

"Yes that's probably wise." Rosanna replied with an element of hurt pride in her voice. Maybe she was offended I didn't trust her plan with my life.

"How is Miss Reed getting on by the way?" I inquire to change the subject.

"Hannah is having a first day from hell, bless her cotton socks." Laughs Rosanna. "She has signed all the paperwork, but you can imagine she is a little concerned her new boss is going to die on the first day." Changing the subject has failed to distract me.

"Haha," I laugh forcefully, "get her to set the camera up and help you draft my speech. She will enjoy getting so involved straight away."

"You got it *boss*." I hate it when Rosanna says that phrase, so cringey. She even adds too much mustard on the word *boss* as she knows it irritates me.

Half an hour later I emerge from my room in a smart black shirt without a tie. I sit in front of the camera set up in the kitchen and Hannah hands me a speech. "Quite a first day," she says but I get the feeling that she is enjoying the drama. I glance through the words written for me and make some adjustments in pencil. Rosanna has placed a chess board behind me on the kitchen counter to my left. I walk over and set up the napoleon attack with a basic Petrov defence against it. Rosanna adjusts the pieces, so they are dead centre in each square and then positions the board so that it is obviously visible on camera.

We have agreed a slot on the afternoon news with Amanda Buckle to provide this statement. With a little shake of the head and a clear of the throat, we are off.

Good Afternoon,

My name is Rowan Schofield, and I am proud to be one of the councillors of North Yorkshire. I am even more proud to be the instigator of the mental health reform legislation and to have improved business in the North Yorkshire region. I love my county, above all else.

With that in mind I am here today to explain my recent challenge to Councillor Jones. Councillor Jones has been a thorn in my side since I took office. This is a woman who rose to power for power's sake. She has no interest in bettering the lives of people in our community and has consistently opposed legislation and ideas which would benefit everyone.

Believe me, I have tried to reason with her. I have tried to compromise and even begged her to take the people's side. She is resolute in her selfishness. Late last night, I could take it no more. I saw Katherine's example and wanted to emulate her prowess. With Councillor Jones out of council we will progress as a county. We will become what we always should have been, prosperous.

I recognise that I may lose tonight and there would be implications if I were to do so. So, I ask, you the citizens of this great county, that if I die you will hold the council to account and continue to improve the lives of people with mental health illnesses in our community.

We fade the video out with some patriotic music, and I get the thumbs up from Rosanna, but Hannah is expressionless.

"I think we should shoot that again. The ending isn't snappy enough." Hannah says. I review the speech and I agree with her. "You should end with a call to arms."

"Spoken like a true soldier." I laugh.

"Ok how about a patriotic statement? Or an inditement of West Yorkshire?" She ignores my joke and continues her train of thought.

"I think a comment which grabs people's attention and shows your intentions would do some good for our cause." Rosanna backs Hannah up. They have been working together for less than a day and they are already thick as thieves. Rosanna has vindicated her interview style.

"What about: North Yorkshire Forever?" Says Hannah.

"Too cringey, I think." Says Rosanna who was deep in thought.

"How about this: I am willing to give my life for my county, the greatest county in Yorkshire?" I ask.

"That sounds like you have already given up, as if you expect to lose." Rosanna is shooting down ideas left, right and centre.

"Fine, well you come up with an idea then." I say with irritation.

"I think he should make a fist and put it next to your heart. Then say, 'North Yorkshire.'" Rosanna is very pleased with her suggestion.

"That's a great idea, it's a symbol that your supporters can mimic in future." Says Hannah who is obviously enjoying her new job. I like the idea too.

We re-record and I place more emphasis on the North Yorkshire aspects of the speech. As I close I make a fist and plant it side-on to the left of my chest. Rosanna and Hannah mimic the gesture as

I do it and I feel the rush of solidarity. This could be huge. So long as I survive the night.

Rosanna checks that the chess board is visible throughout the message and then sends it to YTV news. This is it. Let's see if she takes the bait.

Chapter Sixteen: Chess Hall of Fame

We arrive early and this time I sit at table 14 in preparation for the duel. The chess hall has stone slabs for a floor, and the walls are coated in paintings celebrating the best of North Yorkshire. Large windows allow the vast gardens to be viewed from every position in the hall, however, the darkness of night has set in now and nothing of the outside world can be seen.

Rosanna is not messing around on her phone for this duel. She stands behind me and studies the unmoved chess board as if she is already playing the game herself. Hannah, a duelling virgin, is walking up and down the hall looking at all the paintings and admiring the hall itself. She is aware of the privilege she has to be here without having to face imminent death and looks a little overwhelmed by the situation, which is exacerbated by the candlelight illuminating her face.

Claire arrives on time. She does not look me in the eye as she positions herself on the opposite side of the board. Matthew uses his fingers to swear at Rosanna, Rosanna uses her mouth to swear back. I feel quite unsettled. When a councillor is challenged they have the reassurance that they have made it on the council and generally have a superior knowledge of chess. When councillor challenges councillor that reassurance is thrown out of the window. The camera crew have been waiting in the wings and are so excited by this duel that they have come incredibly close to our faces with their cameras. Matthew returns with the officiator and the chess clocks are started.

This is the moment of truth; will Rosanna's tactic have paid off? Claire's hand hovers over the King's pawn. She is definitely hesitant. As she withdraws her hand from above the pawn she sends a glance my way, she grasps her king's knight and gingerly places it towards the centre of the board. She watched my speech; she has changed her usual opening. Rosanna turns around from the board and I hear her breathe a sigh of relief. We have the upper hand from the start, Claire is playing on unfamiliar terms.

I should not get ahead of myself, just because she is not familiar with this opening does not mean she cannot play it. Furthermore, I have spent the day preparing to deal with the Napoleon Attack. I may have the initial advantage, but that advantage is vanishingly small. It does not take long for Claire's plan to take shape. Within ten moves she has established a King's Indian defence and is waiting for a mistake to capitalise on. I have never seen a councillor play so defensively.

I decide to take some time before making my next move. The game has settled which means I have lost my initial advantage. The atmosphere is stifling, and Rosanna has had to take a break because her hands were trembling. It's true that watching your friend play a duel is much more worrisome than playing it yourself. I close my eyes and try to remember how we were taught to play against the King's Indian defence. It has become an uncommon defensive move of late which is why this was so clever from Claire. The chances of making a mistake on my end have jumped up.

I decide the safest option is to continue my own piece development. I do not feel threatened yet and the more pieces I have in play, the more likely I can break down this problem. I am concerned, nonetheless, that Claire will recognise this move as proof that I am unfamiliar. I change my mind. Moving my black square bishop, I take a free pawn. It has no strategic advantage as the position of the bishop is actually less threatening that it was previously, but it sends a statement. It also wakes the cameraman up who had been looking very bored at the intellectual level of this chess match. He then zooms into Claire's face and gets a fantastic view of her eyebrow raise.

She is confused with that move but evidently she thinks I have some devious plan that she has not thought of, rather than just taking a piece just for the sake of taking it. She spends five minutes of her time glaring at the position of my bishop. I have got under her skin. Rosanna returns looking as pale as an anaemic patient. She is not impressed by my last move but tries not to show it as Claire is panicking about the move for no reason.

Claire finally relaxes having assessed every possible implication of my non-strategic move. She sits back in her chair and breathes a sign of temporary relief. I feel the tension growing in my stomach. This is unbearably tense; I could die tonight. All because I want to be treasurer. Is that really worth it? Why am I in this career? I feel a wave of heat rush over my body and then take up residence in my cheeks. Katherine loses nothing in this transaction, and she could gain a great deal. Let's be honest, I have been manipulated. No wonder Rosanna asked if I was sure, what was I thinking?

I am brought out of my spiralling train of thought by Claire leaning forward and raising her white square bishop in the air. She picks it up and then lets it hang in mid-air. I see her hand trembling, at least I am not the only one who is nervous. She turns to Matthew and whispers into his ear. He stalks of to somewhere or other followed by the irritable gaze of Rosanna. Councillor Jones places her bishop down in a safe, non-threatening position. The chess board remains stagnant.

Move after move, nothing seems to change. I remain one pawn up for at least half an hour before the cameraman finally looks excited. It is my move, but I have no idea why he is excited. Have I got an opportunity, or have I made a mistake? I am about to win or lose? I look for Rosanna out of the corner of my eye, she seems pleased but she does not have much chess experience so that does not tell me much. I place my elbow on the table and rest my head in my hand.

I quickly raise my eyeline to take a glimpse of Claire. Her breathing is much more laboured than before, I think she is trying to calm herself down, I think… It is at this very moment that Matthew returns with a lawyer in tow. I have never seen Matthew look embarrassed before, it is quite a strange sight to behold. He won't look anyone in the eye.

My intrigue at Michael's embarrassment is replaced by intrigue in Claire's embarrassment. She sees Michael and the lawyer, and blushes bright red. She stands up and rushes to them.

She must have made a mistake. Rosanna leans over my shoulder whilst I desperately imagine all the moves I could make and their implications. She whispers, "She called for the lawyer to try and negotiate a truce and maintenance of council positions, she thought she was even."

As both of our teams are swarming around us the chess official came across, seething. "Excuse me! There is to be no collusion during challenges! This is a game between two people, not two teams of people. Sit down miss Jones or I shall declare the game forfeited. The same applies to you, young lady." This last part is directed at Rosanna with the point of a finger.

"I am sorry maam," Claire replies, "would you please recognise Mr Adamshaw here as my lawyer?"

The official nods but adds, "Lawyers are permitted to speak during a game but only in my presence and you know that."

"Yes, of course. My mistake." Claire looks emotionally battered and bruised.

Mr Adamshaw is a well-dressed man. He must be at least six feet tall, and he is wearing a pristine pinstripe suit. He approaches the table, under the beady eye of the official and opens his briefcase. He pulls out a notepad and reads the following statement.

I, Darren Adamshaw, am a lawyer serving for the North Yorkshire county council. I am here today to facilitate negotiations whilst this duel commences. Do all parties consent to my presence?

Claire nods vigorously and dumps her head in her hands. I glance at the board, put on a completely fake smile as if I know what her mistake is, if there is indeed a mistake, and then send a smug smile Claire's way before nodding. In all honesty, duelling sometimes comes down to who acts with the most confidence.

Adamshaw begins the negotiations, the cameras are unbearably close, "I am led to believe by Councillor Jones' team, that she is keen to bring

123

an end to this game before any blood is shed." I listen to the statement and simultaneously check the board for this mistake. Where is it? What can Rosanna see, a non-chess player, that I can't?

Claire is next to speak, "Rowan," I look up, "we shouldn't be doing this. This is insane. Your reasons for challenging we are completely trumped up." Her eyes remind me of a cat begging for food.

"My reasons are perfectly clear." I make a fist and put it to my heart. The camera zooms in on the gesture.

"What are you talking about?" She lets out a noise of disbelief and looks aghast.

I decide to go for it. Why not? If Rosanna is right, she called for the lawyer when she thought she was in control of the match, she doesn't sound like someone confident of victory now.

"I think it's clear I am going to win this match." I declare with a level of arrogance that startles Rosanna. She has to take a sip of water. Claire makes no comment. "Mr Adamshaw, I would like to make my case plain. I will let Miss Jones concede without the death penalty. However, I require her to resign her post and make a

124

commitment never to challenge for office ever again."

Claire is crying now. "I love my county; this job is my life." Matthew has slunk to the back of the room; Rosanna is too nervous to make fun of him right now. I still haven't figured out whatever this mistake she has made is. I am going insane looking for it while pretending I have the upper hand.

She is examining my face with great vigour. Any sign of weakness or lack of confidence and she may decide to play on. All the cameras are turned towards Claire. The pressure is on. Mr Adamshaw intervenes on our silent debate, "Miss Jones, an offer has been made. How would you like to proceed?"

"Please Rowan…" I make every effort to give her no response, verbal or non-verbal. There is a lump in my throat. I think I might cry from the mixture of nerves and guilt of what I am doing to her.

"She extends her arm to me. "I agree to your terms." Tears stream down her face and Matthew is now nowhere to be seen. What a snake, he won't stand by his leader when she is at her lowest ebb. I have no doubt Rosanna will stand by me if I ever lose. I take her hand and the lawyer provides us with documents to sign. I am so thankful there is to be no execution. I am not a murderer nor a soldier.

I just hope Katherine accepts this agreement in lieu of execution. I think she will, she has got what she wanted after all.

As we leave the hall we run into Matthew in the corridor. He is on the phone speaking with someone about job opportunities. Loyalty is a rare thing nowadays. Through the courtyard we are greeted by wild cheers. For the first time in years the courtyard is filled with regular citizens. The journalists attempt to break through their ranks but before they can reach us, our supporters swarm us with adoration.

Hundreds of men and women stand across the walkway, fists held to their chests. I feel like Jesus entering Jerusalem on a donkey. I have to inch my way forward, shaking hands and signing articles of clothing with every step. As soon as the exit is within sight an elderly gentleman blocks the archway. He places a shoebox under his feet and claps his hands to get the crowd to quieten down. A few stragglers fail to get to the message and continue talking but eventually all eyes and ears are turned towards the man.

"I have lived in North Yorkshire all my life." The crowd breaks out into rapturous applause. This was not what the gentleman wanted, and he frantically waves his arms. "I have lived in North Yorkshire all my life." He starts again, "I was here when we gained independence from the English tyranny, I was here when all four counties were declared equal and I have slowly watched as my county, North Yorkshire, has been thrown to the dogs."

You could hear a pin drop in this place.

"Of late, I thought there was no hope." He continues, "Politicians had become progressively more selfish and ignorant. And when councillor Stewart left office I entered an emotional state I can only describe as utter despair." Murmurs of agreement echoed around the outside venue. "That was until I saw this young man. He believes in this county; he believes in his people. This is a man I would gladly follow to war!" At this there was an enormous roar. I do a 360 degree turn and see all these men and women in passionate agreement. This is incredible.

Spontaneously everyone in the place, except the *unbiased* journalists, begin beating their chests with their fists and shouting *North Yorkshire… North Yorkshire…. North Yorkshire…*

Chapter Seventeen: A History Lesson

As we drive home I stare out of the window and write in my official account. Rosanna, Hannah and I are in a mood of disbelief at what we have just seen in the courtyard. I begin to daydream. When I was twelve years old, Councillor Stewart came over for dinner and was sat talking to my parents about the legacy of the civil war. The councillor was much younger then and still had most of his hair. He would come round a lot to see my parents; he had gone to school with my mum. I think it is worth recoding this exchange in my diary as I have never written it down before.

"You are always talking about this war, but no one ever actually tells me what it was about or what happened!" I was a stereotypical enraged 12-year-old boy, in reality I was enraged with the adults in my life for having conversations about things I didn't understand and then never elaborating.

Councillor Stewart was a wise man, and he politely asked my parents if he could have the honour of explaining the story of our nation. It was a weird interaction but that is just the way he was. The story of the revolution was not taught in primary school you see as it was deemed too frightful. My patients agreed with pretend consideration but now I recognise they were as excited to hear him tell the story as I was.

"In 2085," I quickly nod to show that I am following with keen interest, like a student trying to catch the eye of a teacher in a classroom, "there were significant divisions between the North and South of England. England used to be part of a union called the United Kingdom. That meant the union of four countries, England, Scotland, Wales and Northern Ireland."

"In 2035 Scotland left the union. This was after years of referendum and Scottish politicians arguing in its favour. This was a huge blow to the United Kingdom, especially as Northern Ireland were persuaded by the Scottish Independence to try their luck as well and they seceded five years later. That left the United Kingdom as only England and Wales." He gave me a cursory glance to check I understood so far. "Scotland's dissatisfaction had indirectly offered the North of England some minor protections."

"What?" I didn't quite get what he meant by that.

"Well, Scotland constantly held the government to account on certain equality issues. Issues like education funding by location, healthcare spending by location and public transport funding *by location*." I pretend to catch his drift now.

"So, if Scotland kept asking those difficult questions, the government has to distribute money evenly to all areas of the country?" I asked.

"Absolutely right! Your son catches on quickly." My parents both blushed with pride but it was flattery for friendships sake. "So, when Scotland left, and then Northern Ireland left, nobody was asking those questions. And what was worse, the United Kingdom had lost a large part of the economy, which meant they had all the more reason to stop dividing money evenly and focus it on the areas that made the most tax revenue."

"London." I say.

"Well done. Right again! London was the capital of England and had been given a lot of money to invest for many years. The North on the other hand, had been given less money. This meant that when an entrepreneur wanted to start a business they had a choice to make: Start in London with top quality infrastructure, the fanciest houses, the best healthcare, highly educated employees and

130

with political support or start in the North which was cheaper, but which had fewer healthcare providers, poor infrastructure, a lack of highly educated employees available and lower quality housing. Where would you choose Rowan?"

"London."

"And so did all the other entrepreneurs. But this just made things worse, Rowan. More and more money went south, less and less money went North. The south got richer; the north got poorer. Clever people in the North moved down south to make more money, people in the south who could not find work went North to survive on cheaper food and housing. People were desperate but the government didn't care because London and the South was in boom."

"So, we went to war." I say with, what is on reflection, the naive pride of a schoolboy about fighting wars.

"It's not quite that simple," he laughs, "Yorkshire is not the only place in the North." My parents start laughing as well, which was very belittling, and I got a little defensive if I recall correctly.

"Yorkshire was a county back then, not a country. But as a county it was very patriotic. We were known as God's own county and to be honest, other counties didn't like how much we liked our own home." I felt patriotic just hearing about this stuff. "It was because of this patriotism that the people of Yorkshire felt able to stand up to the North-South divide."

"The political system in those days was called democracy. People would go to a box and put a vote in to say who they wanted to represent their area in government. Every five years, political parties, that means groups, put members up for election. The party with the most members were in charge of the country." I was familiar with democracy. We had been taught about Scottish politics in Year 7.

I remember closing my eyes to get my head around this weird system and then open them once I have a grasp on the situation. But this was all for show, I knew about democracy but I wanted to get more complements from the councillor by making him think I had just thought about it. "So why didn't the north vote for people who would favour the north and reduce the divide?"

"An excellent question, really excellent Rowan, I am very impressed. The answer is that they thought they were. In every election the political parties would pretend to care about the north and then when in government they would not change anything. If you voted for a candidate who was not of a major party, they would not have enough support across the country to change anything either. We were stuck in a rut. Nothing would change."

A wave of sadness washed over me.

"On the 28th January 2083, they cancelled all the trains running into Yorkshire for *maintenance* and didn't get them up and running again for five weeks! On the 14th of March they reduced the unemployment cheques to half of what people on unemployment benefit received in the South. They defended this by saying the cost of living, how much money you need to live, was less in the North. Exactly one month later, St James' hospital in Leeds collapsed under financial pressures. This was the last straw. The 15th of April 2083 is when the revolution began."

I was so excited! It was like hearing about your parents winning a competition.

"One woman stood on a street in Richmond. Her five-year-old daughter stood by her side holding her hand. In her other hand she held a sign. It read:

This is not fair. We would be better on our own.

Within hours every major street in Yorkshire was filled to overflowing with angry people. One woman disillusioned with the government had become hundreds of thousands refusing to condone to the United Kingdom's rule.

"Who was the leader?" I ask

"Spoken like a true leader!" I really liked councillor Schofield. "There was no leader. This was a revolution of pure intentions. The people were united in disgruntlement. Together Yorkshire defied the government. Together they closed down all the motorways and train stations and made their own little borders with garden huts as security posts. Of course, there were people who disagreed or agreed slightly too much. But on the whole, the people worked together. That was, until the British Army got involved."

"What happened then?" I remember feeling excited because I knew Yorkshire won.

"They arrived on boats off the coast of Flamborough head in East Yorkshire. They wandered ashore and shot the elderly man managing a little border desk on the port. This was seen by a passer-by who sounded the alarm to the
134

nation. They killed an elderly man, Rowan. For no reason. They were monsters with no restraint. It was at this point that our leadership developed. Four friends met together, one from each of our counties and they formed a plan."

"They were called the Yorkshire Nationalist Party. YNP." At this point Councillor Stewart rolled up his sleeve and across his upper arm tattooed in bold font were the words *YNP 41st Battalion*. "YNP released one statement which said they would give their lives to become independent, any government which kills the elderly is no government of ours. We all answered the call. We fought in East Yorkshire and we fought in South Yorkshire. We won for one reason, we wanted it more. These British soldiers were only there because they were ordered to be there, we were there because we had something to fight for."

"So, this YNP… were they the ones who came up with chess politics?" I had asked so many questions by this point, but the councillor was not getting irritated.

"That's right. Do you know why?" He gave me an opportunity to show off, but I had no idea.

"No." It didn't make any sense to me in all honesty.

"They needed a system where there were no political parties. We hated political parties. The people also believed that democracy had failed them, there was no point in returning to that system as the public wouldn't support it. Therefore, YNP held a conference and proposed an intelligence based political system. It seemed hairbrained to me when I first heard it. They said chess was a good idea and proposed the system we have today, equal education and duels to the death."

"You may wonder why we agreed, was there not a better way of measuring intelligence? IQ tests were ruled out because they didn't offer a duelling aspect. They needed people to fight for their beliefs. We had realised this on Flamborough beach when we were fighting the British, people should only be entrusted with power if they were willing to fight and die for it."

"Chess was chosen because it was a game of pure intellect, no physical aspects were required which would unfairly disadvantage anyone. It was also incredibly fair as a game, there is no luck involved."

The way councillor Stewart presented the chess system to me made it sound reasonable and fair. I am not sure I quite believe that anymore. That is a debate for another day.

When we arrive back at the Octagon I am jolted out of my daydream. That elderly man on the soapbox in the courtyard had reminded me of the elderly man who died at Flamborough beach that day. Maybe all revolutions are started by the old to benefit the young.

Chapter Eighteen: Treasurer at Last

It is gone 1am when Katherine finally calls. We are all lying on my sofas talking about childhood dreams. Hannah says she always wanted to be a soldier, typical and not surprising. Rosanna hasn't said much at all but is listening intently. My phone starts buzzing on the coffee table and we all sit up straight in a flash.

I let it ring a little to make it seem like I haven't been up waiting with bated breath. Katherine is on the other end of the line.

"Well… politicians never could follow orders." She says to open the conversation.

"Well, I am not a murderer." I say with righteous indignation disguising my knowledge of a deal broken.

"You're clearly not a warrior either." She is laughing down the line.

"Can I assume, from this late-night call, that you have accepted my adjustment to our agreement, and I am to be treasurer after all?" This is greeted with stone cold silence.

"Have you ever heard for the term *the spirit of an agreement*?" This was not the clear-cut answer I was looking for.

"No, I have not." I let out some frustration with this retort.

"It means technicalities of an agreement may not be the essential aspect. For example, I could agree not to buy any sweets and then buy mints and claim they are technically different. That would be true, but it would not be in the *spirit of the agreement*."

"In your case, the opposite is true. I asked you to remove Claire and execute her. You removed her and got an agreement that she would never run for office again. You failed the technicalities but obeyed the spirit. With that in mind, it would be my honour to ask you to assume the position of *King's piece* on North Yorkshire county council."

A wave of relief breaks across my face and my companions in the room sense the mood shift. They begin to celebrate in hushed tones. A
139

champagne cork hits the roof and is met with stifled giggles.

"Thank you Katherine, I look forward to furthering our partnership." I place the phone on the hook and then go absolutely Berserk with glee. We celebrate like we are in university again; champagne is flowing, and the music is booming. All the pressure of the last few months seems to have dissipated; it was all worth it. Being treasurer means I have control of the economic situation. Being *King's piece* brings me a step closer to my aim of a free and liberated North Yorkshire.

We are up all night partying. On reflection this was a little premature, we were partying like we had finished our school exams again and were about to head on a summer holiday. This situation was not the same, I was to go to work on Monday morning with more responsibilities than I had ever had in my life. This morning, with a splitting headache, I awake with a keen sense of reality. I won't have a weekend off again until I either retire or die.

I stagger to the bathroom and vomit. I haven't been hung over like this since university. On return to my bed, I put the TV on and turn the volume down low. Sometimes I need the white noise as a distraction when I feel ill, otherwise I just think about how ill I am and end up feeling worse. I drift off to sleep again.

I am woken up horribly by Rosanna who bursts through the door and starts jumping on my bed. Is she still drunk from last night?

"All the dominoes are falling into place! Good news follows good news!" Rosanna shouts breathlessly between jumps. I have never seen her this excited, but I honestly don't want to hear it right now so I roll over and curl up in child's pose.

"Get up you idiot!" She has taken my shoulders and is shaking me like I have passed out in hospital and the doctors are trying to see if I am responsive.

"What?" This word is more grunt than pronunciation.

"Professor Odoi messaged me this morning. He wants us to drive to Scarborough and meet him tonight. He says he has good news." She is way too jubilant for a Saturday morning.

I pass out again.

Chapter Nineteen: University Discussions

I am feeling better this afternoon and I have asked Hannah to stay in Harrogate and figure out the exact statistics regarding the mental health unemployment benefit claims. I need to know how much the county is haemorrhaging each month because of my reform. I expected Hannah to be disappointed at not being invited to Scarborough but like a true soldier she took the order and got to work straight away without a word of complaint.

Rosanna says we have to be discreet for some reason. When she has a plan, she likes to leave it to the last minute before she informs me of the exact details. I think she just wants as much time as possible to brood on it and make sure it works in her head. We get into her blue classic mini. It has a melted clockface in the centre of the dashboard where the radio would normally sit. I absolutely love this car, it sums up Rosanna's personality as well, time is more important than a radio.

Scarborough, alongside most seaside towns, had been wildly neglected by the UK but had become a major hub of activity post revolution. Whitby and Scarborough have become the fishing supplier of the country and the main route of major imports. As a result, the promenade has been completely regenerated and the houses have been transformed. I am a little startled when we arrive at the university, it is so grand that I feel out of place. This is one of the centres of academia in our county. I am walking on hallowed ground and hopefully the Professor has a gift from God for me.

Rosanna parks her treasured car in a multi-story car park, and we take the lift down to the main entrance of the *John Snow* medical school building. Once we are sat in the reception, a modern building with an open plan area and free tea and coffee, Rosanna looks ready to talk. She gives me a cursory glance to make sure I am in the mood to listen and whispers,

"I think we both know he has developed a treatment due to us funding his research." I hesitantly agree with some vague noises, I have been trying not to get my hopes up. "If that is the case, we need to make the treatment only available to North Yorkshire citizens." I am horrified at Rosanna's plan and I can't help but screw my face into a strange cotorsion.

143

"That's monstrous! What kind of morals would we have if we prevented people across Yorkshire, across the world for that matter, from getting a treatment which could change their lives for the better?" I ask in disgust.

"I have thought about that argument! But on the flip side of the coin, what kind of morals would we have if we risked our lives for a policy to help our citizens, and then as soon as it comes good, we give all the profits away and reduce the potential benefits for our own people."

"You're going to have to elaborate on that." I am aware of my own stubbornness, but I feel pretty confident I am in the right on this view.

"Look, I can see you're riled up. Take a deep breath. Just listen to the logic, without judgement and tell me the flaw." I take a huge breath. "North Yorkshire develops a cure for anxiety and depression and limits the supply to their own citizens. Within a few months, sick days have disappeared saving businesses millions, more work and more productivity means more spending and more exports, *the economy becomes stronger than ever before*." She says these last few words very slowly.

"Within a year North Yorkshire will become an economic hub which would give us the power we need to usurp the West. The people of North Yorkshire, *the people we represent* will be liberated from the bondage of both mental illness and poverty."

"When would you roll out the treatment to the rest of the world?" I ask.

"Once, North Yorkshire has secured its position. A month of economic boom and then we give it out. Otherwise, we would be monsters." She states with unbearable calmness.

We are interrupted by a nice man in a sharp looking suit, clearly a recent university graduate, with scruffy stubble lining his chin line. He politely provides us with guest ID badges and walks us to the laboratory on the third floor. Through multiple double doors with ID scanners, we eventually find our room. Professor Odoi is awaiting us, he is dressed in a white coat and is fiddling with a presentation that he is projecting on an old overhead projector.

When he notices us through the glass he jumps out of his seat and makes a massive deal of welcoming us and sitting us on leather padded chairs. He is the stereotypical eccentric scientist,

145

right down to his slightly wonky wide framed glasses.

We sit in an awkward silence with a simultaneous electric atmosphere. Professor Odoi is unable to sit still. He kindly informs us that he is waiting for the other researchers to arrive.

"I would also like to add; I know you took a great leap of faith, at great personal risk, and I am grateful for the funding and trust you have placed in me and my team." The professor has an amazing Yorkshire accent.

"You are very welcome; it is about time someone took a stand for those in need." I reply.

The professor sees through my political style answer and gives me a quizzical smile in response. The tense awkwardness envelops the room once more until a series of men and women dressed in white coats enter with a bustle. An elderly lady boots up the PowerPoint and we are off.

The professor is on his feet in a flash, lazerpoint pen in hand and glasses on the edge of his nose. He picks up a small blue pill and unfurls his hand in front of our faces. The pill has a RS engraved in the centre. "In honour of you, for believing in us." I

146

feel myself blush; this is more personal than any political statement I could make in reply.

"This tablet is the comprehensive key to biological variant anxiety and depression. We have used the SSRIs monoamine hypothesis and adapted it to ensure a perfect correction of serotonin replacement needed for each individual patient."

"Mate, I am no scientist! Pretend I am your patient and explain it that way." I am baffled.

"Ahahaha, good idea," he is too happy to be bothered by my ignorance, "Mr Schofield, we are going to take a sample of your brain fluid, this means putting a needle into your spine and removing some fluid. It is called a lumbar puncture. We will use that fluid to analyse the serotonin content in your brain. Serotonin is a messenger in your brain which can be linked to anxiety and depression. If you have a low concentration we will provide you with pills to correct this. This will improve your symptoms." He is clearly giddy at his explanation; I get the feeling he hasn't practiced medicine with patients for many years.

"Ok, I think I am getting it. There is a marker in my brain chemistry which can tell you if I am depressed or not. Like how a blood test tells you how much sugar is in my blood." I say with drawing on my school science.

"It is not quite that simple but yes." I am worried his smile will become so broad his ears will fall into his mouth.

"How effective is it?" I need to know the nitty gritty before I give this pill my backing. I am worried my initials on the tablet was just a move to butter me up.

"The trails we have conducted showed a 100% improval in symptoms in patients with biological depression and anxiety. We defined improval as a reduction in frequency or severity of symptoms reported by each individual patient. 82% reported a complete loss of symptoms. Upon removal of treatment all patients returned to their previous mental state."

"Wow that does sound good." I turn to Rosanna, giving her licence to open up her line of questioning.

"Biological depression and anxiety? Why do you keep adding the term biological?" She asked without hesitation, that question has been brewing for some time I deduce.

"That is a very astute question." The professor is looking at Rosanna as if he wants to place a white coat around her shoulders and pay her very little for working harder than she works now. "The answer is complex. You see, there are some people in the world who would have developed anxiety or depression no matter what environment they had grown up in. For example, if they had lived in a house with millionaire parents, the greatest education in the world and the greatest doctors, they would still have developed mental illness. These patients do also present in terrible housing, in poverty and with useless doctors."

"There are also patients who would not have developed symptoms if something in their life had been avoided. For example, the patient who was on holiday as a child and almost drowned may develop a mental illness that they would not have developed otherwise. It is these patients who are non-pharmacologically possible to treat. They need talk therapy. We call those, experiential mental illness."

"To put it simply: biological mental illness can be treated with medication or talk therapy and preferably both. Those with experiential mental illness will only respond to talk therapy." He has an expression which reminds me of my high school teacher.

"This treatment you are proposing will only help a proportion of people with mental illness?" Rosanna has a keen understanding of public health and epidemiology.

"Correct." He says.

"What proportion do you estimate that to be?" She is straight to the point.

"It is hard to say exactly as it depends on the region. Poorer areas, sadly, will have a higher percentage of experiential mental illness than more well-off areas. We estimate around 60% are biological. The only way to treat the other 40% is to improve living conditions and provide comprehensive talk therapy to those still affected." This is a political mine field now.

"If we licence this pill, I would be another politician improving the lives of the rich ahead of the poor." I am deeply saddened by this revelation and am praying for a good answer from the professor.

"I understand your frustration." He says with sympathy, but he has already prepared an argument. "However, I disagree with your premise. If we treat all those with biological mental illness then we will also treat many poor people. Poor people have biological mental illness too remember. Furthermore, this will also allow us to identify those who need talk therapy the most and we can prioritise them for treatment. We will be shining a light onto the effects of inequality in our country and that will spark a nationwide recognition that things need to change."

"Spoken like I politician." I say as I rock back and forth in my chair and appreciate his logic. "We have known for a long time that inequality is bad, but we haven't really changed anything yet."

"That's your job not mine." Professor Odoi retorts sharply.

Chapter Twenty:
Announcements

The afternoon proceeds with a laboratory visit, further discussions about classifications of mental illness and a constant theme of wild excitement from the Professor. I am beginning to catch the excitement from him. This is a really huge deal and basically vindication of my mental health reform. I do have some concerns about the effectiveness, maybe I didn't understand how complex mental illness was before I embarked upon this adventure.

The professor has made a strong argument, nonetheless. The psychiatric health budget would be much more accommodating for patients with experiential anxiety and depression. They would get all the talk therapy they need rather than the insufficient therapy that every patient gets at the moment. It is without question that this treatment needs to be offered to the population, which leads me on to a more pressing issue, Rosanna's proposal.

I decide the best course of action would be to discuss this plan with the Professor, having a scientific excuse to only provide treatment to North Yorkshire citizens first would keep the council out of trouble with the West and ease my conscience as well. It takes a long time for me to divert the Professor's attention from his tour and eventually we get him into a side room to talk.

There is no doubt that this man is a genius and within seconds he reaffirms that to us. His demeanour has changed from the excitable man we had met before to an intensely discerning man with no time for politics. Before we have said a word he interjects,

"I have no time for games, I have no time for politics. I took your research grant because, for once, I thought you were different. But low and behold, I am being shoved in a side room, I presume to give you some excuse to do something that will help your career." He is stern, sterner than I thought capable from the childlike man I had met two hours ago.

This needs to be de-escalated fast. "I quickly became aware of how rare it is for you to take a meeting with a politician and I would not dream of abusing that trust and level of communication that we have. I want to roll out this drug, fast. I presume you have called because it has passed all the trial standards?"

He is partly assuaged by my interest in his pharmacology but not completely placed at ease. "We have completed stage two trials which tells us that our drug is safe and effective. We are now looking at manufacturing on mass, safe distribution and training of healthcare professionals."

"That is exactly what I wanted to hear. Is there any way we can limit this distribution to North Yorkshire alone?" I say casually.

He folds his arms, glowers and begins to mutter under his breath. We are stood in silence for a seconds before he speaks once more, "Let's remove politics for a second. Just be honest with me, I am a clinician by trade, I know when a patient is lying. What do you gain from North Yorkshire only distribution?"

"I, hopefully, gain political power for North Yorkshire which I can use to offset the imbalance within our country and improve the lives of my citizens." I say with a level of honesty which makes me uncomfortable.

"Distributing this drug to the world fulfils my goal of improving people's lives. I would say the number of lives improved by providing this medicine to the world would be more than there are citizens in North Yorkshire." We are now in a debate; I feel like I am back in debate society in University.

"I agree, however, I think you can do even more for people in the future if you live in a county which provides you with the money you need for research in other areas of medicine, I think you have a level of patriotism which you are hiding and I know you are aware that there are people in your life, whom you love, who are adversely affected by the state that we live in. It is undebatable that more people will benefit from this medicine being offered around the world, but let me reiterate, it will be offered around the world, just with a slight delay. You can do so much good with this drug, you can do better if you play politics, just this once, and give it to North Yorkshire first."

The professor contemplates my improvised speech for quite some time. I pop my head out of the door and politely ask for some coffee to be brought to our little side room. We haphazardly sit on poorly spaced chairs and await the professor's ruminations to come to a close. He sips his coffee every so often but aside from that we have no indication of any brain activity.

It is quite some time before the professor places his elbows on his knees and opens his mouth. He is holding his cup of coffee firmly in both hands.

"Did you know my father served in the revolution?" I was genuinely unaware of this fact and I shook my head. I would have used that as a bargaining chip if I had known.

"My family fled from Sri Lanka. I wasn't born yet but the Sri Lankan civil war is burnt into my heart from the impact it had on my family. They say your heritage is not important when you've lived in another culture your whole life. Those people are very wrong. Those people are never related to migrants or asylum seekers."

Rosanna and I are desperate to pay him as much respect as humanly possible in this moment. We both know this was a moment which may be extremely beneficial for us if we play our cards right. We instantaneously recognise that the professor seldom speaks of these events in his life, it was an honour to be in his presence when he did so.

"When we arrived here, under rights provided to us by our commonwealth status, we were greeted with unprecedented hostility. People did not understand the horrors we had fled. Tamil people were going missing in their thousands, Sinhalese people were being blown to pieces by the inventors of the suicide bomb. We ran because we had to and yet we were the ones who met with fear and hostility."

"No matter what we said to people or how we behaved we could not get our story across. We could not be welcomed. With that in mind my Father had his ingenious idea. We recognised that there were some migrants who were treated better than others and we are brown people. Most Britons couldn't tell the difference from one brown country to another. So, we changed our surnames." He was crying now, softly.

"To fit in we changed our surnames. People in London knew our original name, so we moved to Yorkshire. We felt like witnesses being held in a police protection scheme. New identities, new lives. But we should never have done it, the people of Yorkshire recognised we were normal, good people. Whenever Sri Lanka was discussed, the people understood it as the tragedy on both sides. They never spoke a word that favoured either the Tamil Tigers or the Sinhalese government. Their only concern was for the innocent people who had been caught up in the middle of it all."

"My father was heartbroken. He had sacrificed our heritage to keep us out of harm's way when all he needed to do was move to Yorkshire. He felt like a traitor to his race and his country. He loved Yorkshire for what it was, he hated the response the rest of the UK had given him. He died in the revolution fighting in Flamborough. I was fifteen." Professor Odoi could not continue any further. He blubbered until he his words could no longer be distinguished.

Amidst the sadness Rosanna softly whispered, "Odoi is not a Sri Lankan name is it, Professor? May I ask, with humility, why you kept the name your Father chose, if it made him so sad?"

The professor broke his cycle of tears with a fleeting smile. "Because I love my Father and respect the sacrifice he made for us. I wear the name he chose with pride. We are so much more than what people said of us."

"Listening to your speech, Mr Schofield, makes me feel conflicted. I am a migrant, I am not from this country and I feel I have a duty to people beyond these borders to improve their lives. At the same stage, my Father gave his life for the liberties and principles that Yorkshire embodies. He loved this place; he would roll in his grave if he saw how North Yorkshire is currently being treated. North

Yorkshire is my home. Therefore, I will, out of respect for my Father, allow you to play your political games. But, let me tell you this young man, you better win."

In my mind I am leaping for the sky with joy, in body I am nodding gently to match the tone of the conversation.

Monday morning, on the steps of the Harrogate International Centre, I stand with Odoi in unison and give the greatest speech of my career so far. All I say is this,

Ladies and Gentlemen,

It is my great privilege to introduce Professor Odoi, who brings tidings of great joy.

The professor takes it from there. He outlines the mental health problem in our great county, the solution he proposes and the roll out of the medication in a succinct speech which leaves me breathless. He recognises that many people will be nervous about taking such a medication, to this he lists his credentials, his previous inventions and the rigorousness of his clinical trial. He ends with this:

I have great news for those thousands of people who deserve great news more than most. I have spent my life looking to help those with mental health illness and I have achieved my goal. For those who want help, I am here. For those who need help, I am here. For those who are nervous about taking any medication for a mental illness, I can assure you that if you were my son or daughter, I would want you on this treatment. This will change your life.

Chapter Twenty One: Immediate Response

The immediate response from the public was indescribable. Even I am astounded, and I have been dreaming of best-case scenarios for months. A lot of credit goes to Rosanna, she has compiled a list of every member of the public who had registered as disabled under our legislation and sent an email invite to a NSSRI hospital clinic as soon as the medication was announced. NSSRI is the technical name of the pill, Non-selective serotonin reuptake inhibitor, although most people call it Schofield's pill.

She had prewritten to the healthcare students of every medical and nursing school in North Yorkshire and asked them to pitch in and help when they had spare time, she paid them next to nothing for the honour of helping run a lumbar puncture clinic. Poor students, they are not allowed to perform the procedure themselves and so they spent their working hours organising the system until it ran like a military operation. It is a good thing for use that students are so broke.

Within one month we had eighty-five percent of people registered with anxiety and depression at a GP practice on our medication. Of the 78,572 people who had registered as unemployed due to mental illness, ninety percent took the medication. We simply could not believe our eyes as we watched the daily updates on the rolling news. It resembled a pandemic but on this occasion it was a pandemic of improving health.

Rosanna is walking around the office with pride. Sometimes she bursts into my room and shouts about how many more people have begun treatment, the next moment I overhear her on the phone telling the administrators that they must not slacken the pace as they have to meet the new deadlines we have set them. Obviously we need all of these patients to have regular check-ups, especially as we are justifying the exclusivity of treatment under the pretence that we are conducting a major research trial with our whole community. I wonder whether those who have not come forward are simply confused about whether they are in a trial or taking an approved drug. Then again, some people wouldn't take medicine regardless of how good it is.

Things are going well but my position as chancellor gives me a prime view of what is going on with the economy and the statistics have not picked up quite yet. I was hoping for a boom, but I have to be patient. The economy never moves quickly… On the other hand, unemployment is starting to fall. It feels ironic as many of the people who had signed up for unemployment, after anxiety and depression had become a disability, have returned to their previous place of employment. They have basically been paid by the government to do nothing for a few months. I am praying every night that the economy shows some of the success that we were expecting, we know the health benefits are on the right track.

Six weeks following the commencement of the treatment scheme we have had an invitation to join Katherine for dinner at Castle Howard. Dinner at Castle Howard is similar to meeting the Queen of England in the old days. It means good news and congratulations. It never means a telling off. I would not enjoy a telling off right now after everything we have achieved, it would feel like a kick in the teeth.

Upon arrival, we know instantly that this was our moment in the sun. Being a black-tie event and the presence of a red carpet has given us this impression. Journalists and Paparazzi stand behind velvet rope and ask us to pause for pictures. It is surreal! We are politicians not singers. I am relieved to see Professor Odoi has also been invited, let's face it, he deserves all the plaudits. He is dressed in a stunning tuxedo but looks like a deer in headlights with all the press surrounding him.

Rosanna in Castle Howard without her duelling dress is a quite frankly odd. She has compensated for this by dressing in the image of a Yorkshire rose. She is in a flowing white dress which has petal-like folds opening towards her face. For once she is pausing to talk to journalists and is conscious of her tone of voice. I am astounded by the change in her demeanour. She must be revelling in the glory of a political victory. We haven't had so many as piece and pawn yet.

The professor has spotted us further down the red carpet and he scampers towards with the clear expression of relief at seeing someone whom he knows. Rosanna is distracted with her adoring paparazzi, so I speak to the Professor.

 "If I thought entering the political world was like this I would never had agreed!" He says with a slight smirk.

"Wait until you do something wrong." I joke back. I divert my eyes for a second and see we have accumulated a following of photographers who love the fact that we are talking to each other like normal people. These pictures will be on the tabloid front covers in the morning; the magazines will have pictures of Rosanna no doubt.

The professor and I are sat opposite one another near the head of the table with Katherine in chief position and her poor pawn at the foot of the table. The First Minister's pawn has to entertain the boring people who are obligatory invites at these events. The table is candle lit and there are no electric lights in the entire banquet hall. Tridents of candles illuminate everyone's faces.

Rosanna is sat further down the table and is opposite Anthony who looks wildly irritated at his position. Serves him right, I am sure Rosanna will be putting needles in him all night. What was it Jesus said about siting at the end of the table to show humility? I am sure he wouldn't have approved of sitting at the bottom of the table and scowling at those above you. Anthony is so snake like he could be Satan.

The meal is more civil than celebratory with more discussion about cinema and TV than politics and mental health. Katherine is a skilled entertainer and has had to host many state dinners, but she seems more relaxed with us, we are some of her own kind, I suppose. The evening resumes at a casual pace with a pianist and an after-dinner speaker, a comedian who makes jokes about people from different areas of Yorkshire. He treads lightly around North Yorkshire I notice.

As the night is nearing its end and people are starting to leave I am struck by the sea of happy faces. It is remarkable how many people will celebrate your success without speaking to you all night. All the councillors seem to think they have had something to do with the success of this tablet, despite desperately trying to stop the legislation. They seem to have forgotten Claire and Esther, I haven't and nor has Katherine.

The true night has begun and the numbers in Castle Howard are starting to dwindle. Soon the room is inhabited by only myself, Rosanna, Katherine, the Professor, Katherine's pawn Michael and Hannah who arrived late due to some paperwork I gave her. I felt bad about that when she turned up midway through the main course. She didn't mind though and accepted my apologies. We are all sat around the top of the banquet table with copious alcoholic drinks around us.

Michael has moved from the bottom of the table to right hand man, and he looks more comfortable here. He has been on duty all night and now he is able to kick loose. Michael is a very small man with wispy hair. He had gone to primary school with Katherine and is her lifelong friend. Aside from that no one knows much about him, apart from that he very rarely speaks out of turn. Meanwhile the Professor is a sober as a monk and enjoying the drunkenness around him. He looks on with glee at us all struggling to keep our eyes open and our words enunciated.

"I am glad you guys are the last to leave." Says Katherine, "I have some interesting news for you all." She is giggling like a madwoman.

"Last night I received my seventh official complaint from West Yorkshire about the availability of medication." She burst out laughing. The laughing was infectious and before long everyone, except the sober professor, was crying with laughter.

"Why is this so funny, may I ask?" Odoi looks quite displeased.

Between bursts of laughter Katherine manages to fumble out the words, "because they suck." Which just make the rest of us laugh even harder. My stomach muscles were really starting to hurt. Nevertheless, the Professor is not amused by the laughter.

"Am I not grasping the situation right or am I incorrect in saying that West Yorkshire is in charge of the country? Are we not under a lot of pressure, more pressure than we can afford to be laughing at?"

The group iss calming down slowly and, aside from a few bursts of sporadic giggling which would set of the chain again, we are able to explain the hilarity of the situation.

"To put it simply, it is funny because they cannot do anything about it. You invented it in North Yorkshire. We gave you grounds to limit the initial use to North Yorkshire alone. It has been a wild success so far. They have no right to interfere because we are claiming that this is a clinical trial organised within North Yorkshire. All scientific research decisions are, by law, decided on a local government level. Therefore, let your hair down and have a good laugh."

"I take it you know what you're doing in the long run." Was all he would say. We didn't care, and Rosanna managed to make him smile after whispering something in his ear.

Chapter Twenty Two:
Three types of lies

Some claim that the former UK Prime minister Benjamin Disraeli invented the phrase, "there are three types of lies: Lies, damned lies and statistics." Whoever said it first, I don't care, all I know is that it is completely true. Hannah has completed the mini project I had assigned her at an incredible pace and the finished product indicates the abuse of statistics which I have suffered from and which I was about to use to my advantage.

We are all excited about the day that lies ahead of us. Press announcement after press announcement, all with the begrudging eyes of journalists who know they can't demonise me whilst I am riding so high on public opinion. So long as I avoid any discriminatory comments I am in the clear.

Our first engagement, as ever, is with Amanda Buckle. Amanda has a deceptively large recording studio in Knaresborough overlooking the River Warf. It is a common discussion amongst interviewees of hers; the trains running across the bridge behind her head can be incredibly distracting. I am sat in her staging room looking at my flashcards, the leather chair is sticking to my sweaty legs. When will Yorkshire realise that just because we have harsh winters doesn't justify lack of aircon in the summer? I see beads of an unknown liquid streaming down the beige walls.

Amanda emerges from a side door with what seems like too much make-up, but I am sure it will look normal when on camera. She is unbelievably tall with jet black hair. She gives me a friendly nod and a short, natural smile. She opens the door to the main studio and beckons me in with an outstretched hand.

The interview chair is as leathery and sweaty as the staging room chair. I feel like I can't move to readjust for fear of the horrible noise it will create. Meanwhile Amanda is sat on this elevated swivel chair which looks like heaven and makes her guest feel inferior with the height difference. On the desk in front of her is a huge pile of notes. I have always found it irritating that journalists can have notes but the second a politician pulls out notes they look unprepared or incompetent.

A tiny man in denim shorts shouts, "live in three," and then uses his fingers to indicate two and one.

A red light begins flashing above the camera and Amanda starts her monologue. Before long she swivels to face me and the camera pans to a wide shot which shows both of us in the frame. In the studio there are live feeds to show you how you look on camera. I subtly push down a bulge in my shirt which is making me look fat.

"Councillor Schofield, I imagine you are feeling fantastic at the moment." She starts.

"Not at all Amanda, every morning I awake with fear that someone who could have their life transformed by this treatment has decided not to take it up for fear or are prevented by lack of access to healthcare." This is a brazen lie; I have never felt so confident in my career.

"It is interesting you bring up lack of access to healthcare." Oh no, I think, and then panic that my face is portraying my discomfort on camera. "There are wild conspiracy theories from the other counties that this drug is only available to the people of North Yorkshire because you and Councillor Tyne want to usurp West Yorkshire's political influence."

"Those conspiracy theories are astoundingly false. Councillor Tyne and I are passionate about North Yorkshire, the past few months have shown what we are willing to sacrifice for our people. Do not forget, both of us faced challengers this winter and councillor Tyne had to remove a corrupt chancellor to protect our citizens. Nevertheless, we would never do anything that did not have the best interests of our nation as a whole at heart." Lies, lies and more lies. I haven't even got to the statistics yet, hopefully dropping the word *chancellor* will move the conversation towards more familiar turf.

"Let's talk about that corruption." She continues. "What evidence is there that Esther was corrupt, and what about Claire? Was she corrupt as well? Or were you just angling for a promotion?" She hit the nail on the head here but asking the right question will not give her the answer she is looking for.

"I am grateful you have brought this up Amanda," must use her name as many times as possible to make myself personable, "As King's piece I have seen the statistics first-hand and can elaborate with your viewers as to how our people were being deceived! It absolutely disgusts me what Esther did whilst in office. Let me be crystal clear, I do not speak ill of the dead for no reason."

Amanda is enjoying my little piece of dramatic theatre and widens her eyes with delight at the apparent controversy.

"Esther manipulated data like a mastermind. I am sure you remember, Amanda, not long ago when I was still black square rook that there were daily stories about the rapidly climbing unemployment numbers in relation to my legislation regarding mental illness as a disability."

"Yes of course, the statistics were very frightening to many tax paying citizens." She recollects correctly.

"Well, they were grossly exaggerated. Esther took every form in the department of work and employment and assessed them for the any mention of mental health difficulties. If she found any unemployed person who who had mentioned mental health, she would reassign them as unemployed due to mental health disability, even if they were unemployed for other significant factors." I am hoping this statement is clearer to the viewer than it is in my head.

"Let me just get my head around what you are saying." She pauses, "this means that the reduction in unemployment that we are currently seeing is even more impressive than suggested."

God I love Amanda Buckle!

"Absolutely! Not only are those with certified mental health disabilities returning to work in huge numbers, but productivity has increased as a county, meaning those on unemployment benefits not directly related to mental health are finding more employment opportunities. We are on the cusp of a major economic boom and the average North Yorkshire citizen has prosperity coming to them in the near future." I have laid it on a little thick now, but I am in the groove. I have also done a smidge of exaggerating but now I am chancellor no one has access to the data that I have.

"I would like to ask you about your personal aspirations for a moment." I am already preparing the classic response of *I have no aspirations for power* when she alters the question a little, "Sorry let me rephrase that, I want to ask you about the aspirations you have for North Yorkshire." I am temporarily dumbfounded. Paralysed between thoughts of telling the open and honest truth to try and insight some revolutionary spirit or denying my dreams as the people are not quite ready yet for such a hard-hitting message yet.

There is a palpable pause in the recording studio and the summer heat begins to aggravate me once more.

"That is a very difficult question for me to quantify. In simple terms I want North Yorkshire to be the best that it can be."

"Well obviously, but what specifically does that look like to you?" She is tightening her grip on this question and I must answer, or I'll be the laughingstock on some 12-year-old's video on *Youtube* entitled with a phrase about me being destroyed, ruined or obliterated.

"It means being able to run our county with the respect of the other counties. It means getting York back from those East Yorkshire thieves, it means having decent services for our people and not losing our best staff to West Yorkshire. It means rewarding the people who have given their lives to improve their local community, not the rats who jumped ship at the hint of money. It means liberation from tyranny." By the end of my outburst my voice is so loud I can see the sound technician moving the microphone boom away from me. I've let the cat out of the bag now, let's hope people back me up. Otherwise, I am in deep, deep trouble.

"Sounds reasonable to me." Amanda says. I look back at the camera man to see if she has actually said that on air. The red light is now off. Personal support, I need public support. I thank her anyway and walk out into the summer breeze. The hot air does not give me the relief I want so I guzzle a bottle of Harrogate Spa water and walk down a winding pavement to get closer to the river.

Chapter Twenty Three:
By The Riverside

Drinking a *Coca-Cola* in an immature effort to remind me of my previous successes whilst simultaneously trying to cool myself down, I become acutely aware of my surroundings. Upon the hill, Knaresborough Castle overlooks the river. It is covered in posters, there are some inconsequential posters about gentrification of the high street and one teenager has clearly tried to make a professional looking poster to promote legalisation of weed. However, one little clusters of posters about mental health catch my eye.

They seem to have formed a new catch phrase, *the left behind*, they are calling themselves. Some have mental health conditions like OCD, ADHD and bipolar whilst others say they have tried the tablet we are offering to no avail. I think back to the conversation with Professor Odoi in that laboratory so secluded from reality, experiential depression and anxiety, he had called it. Not pharmacologically suitable for treatment he had said. These are people not lab rats.

I take a seat on a bench and watch the ducks squabbling over bread being thrown in by a family downstream. Canada geese roam the waters with great authority and decide to chase the ducks away. They are so ravenous they eventually scare the family feeding them away by getting out of the water and waddling towards them. Don't bite the hand that feeds you as they say.

I see some children getting ice cream and the lawn in front of mother Shipton's cave is awash with band stands and children's fairground games. The sound of children playing brightens the air but the subconscious *Left Behind* statement cannot be torn asunder. Sitting on the hill speaking to all below, *We are the left behind, what about our mental health?*

"I thought I might find you here." Says a familiar voice behind me. I turn to find Katherine in a summer dress with a look of consternation on her face. It is peculiar to see Katherine out and about without guards or advisors. Maybe she thinks the same on seeing me.

She motions towards the rowing boats tied to the shoreline, "fancy a row?"

Without answering I accompany her to the waterside and attempt to hire a boat. The school-aged summer intern looks at us in awe rather than taking my money and eventually his manager comes over and gives us the boat for free for 'as long as we could ever need.'

Katherine has now placed her oversized sunglasses on and steps onto the boat with the assistance of an outstretched hand from the manager of the rowing boats. He offers the same treatment for me but my pride kicks in and I clamber aboard a little clumsily of my own volition. I row us out into the middle of the river, and we follow the flow down to a small waterfall where buoys tell us not to row any further. At this point Katherine stops looking at the scenery and states,

"I saw the interview Rowan. You were quite the passionate schoolboy in there."

I sit in silence and watch the ducks again. They seem different when you are also on the water, much more skilful in their wanderings.

"One thing you said did get my attention however, York." She is now looking at the scenery too. "Although I would caution you, my friend, about invoking such emotion in yourself. Emotions are powerful when directed for good, but they can easily spiral out of control and cause great harm."

Again, I sit in silence and await my verdict from the dispatch box. The heat has dissipated across the water and I can feel myself relaxing. This pause lasts a long time. Katherine has also been distracted by the bickering ducks and it is not until they swim into the reeds that she returns to her thoughts.

"I would like to make a deal with the East Yorkshire County Council." She says bluntly. Her words are like a knife into my chest.

"That would fly in the face of everything we agreed. Moreover, we do not need to do it!" I splutter.

"What did I say about emotions?" She asks with a wry smile.

"Of course, you want to follow the diplomatic path. Let me guess, give them access to the NSSRIs in return for York. That is not a display of strength, that is weakness pure and simple. WEAKNESS!"

"I want York back. Whatever it takes." She replies calmly. "Even if it annoys my fellow council members." That last sentence overflows with patronising connotations.

I take a deep breath and glance at the waterfall to collect my thoughts. "OK, emotions aside." I take another deep breath to emphasise my change in tone. "I want York back too, but why should we trade our stronger hand when we can simply take it back by demand."

"Nice to see you again *logic*, please elaborate." The patronising continues.

"Any glance at our history books will show you the significance of public opinion in our county. We have fought wars over it. There is so much respect for public opinion in Yorkshire simply because the world knows Yorkshire men and women back up their views with actions. I wonder, if a poll was to be taken, what the views of people in York are? I wonder if they identify as North Yorkshire or East Yorkshire? I wonder if their opinions may have been swayed recently."

"That's an awful lot of 'what ifs.' Trading is guaranteed." Katherine argues.

"Guaranteed officially yes. But York citizens aren't going to respect us for buying them back. They will resent us, see us as weak. I want North Yorkshire to be reunited with a long-lost friend, not forced into the back of a car with a Pitbull." I am proud of the argument I have laid out now.

Katherine does not respond but takes hold of the oars and gently glides us back towards the dock. I see Hannah standing with a massive ice cream in her hand watching us like I had watched the Canada geese. Interest mingled with respectful fear. The sun is beating down on our little boat but it is only as we reach the shore I feel the heat return.

Katherine removes the flake from the ice cream with her teeth and devours it whole. "There is always a deal to be done. For now, I will do a deal with you. I will give you three months to stage your miniature revolution. After three months, deals will take place in the East."

I nod and walk away with Hannah. Challenge accepted.

Chapter Twenty Four:
First Time for Everything

On return to the Octagon, I am taken in by a furious Rosanna. She narrows her eyes at me, and her fists are clenched.

"What's the matter with you?" I ask, matching the level of hostility I am receiving from Rosanna. This was a mistake and only furthers the strange atmosphere. I can honestly say Rosanna has never been like this with me.

"I saw your interview, which I was not happy with… and then… I am informed by text…" The words are now coming through gritted teeth with a sharp biting tone, "that you have made a little deal with Katherine… without speaking with me but speaking with Hannah."

At the mention of her name Hannah edges towards the door and places a hand on the door handle. She is halted by Rosanna who uses her palm to tell her to stop moving whilst still glaring at me.

"I am hoping, nay I am expecting that I have got the wrong end of the stick." Rosanna closes her opening statement with an invitation to conciliation.

I make a conscious effort to show sincerity in my body language. I unfold my arms and make an attempt at puppy eyes. "I would never do anything without your knowledge! I did make a deal," Rosanna's body language is becoming more and more closed, "but it was a forced deal. She took me out on a rowing boat and told me she was going to trade our success to East Yorkshire in return for York."

"That's actually a reasonable deal." She raises her eyebrows in surprise. "We did say we would be handing out NSSRIs to the rest of the world very soon, in fact we are later than what we originally promised to Odoi, months late."

"I didn't agree to that deal. I made a different deal; I think we can get York back without trading anything. I think the people of York want to be North Yorkshire now, especially now that we have an added incentive."

"Wait what? Are your trying to start an insurrection?"

"Not an insurrection, minor civil unrest leading to a referendum."

"Oh, for goodness' sake. You are such a coward!" I recoil with hurt. "Have you never read the chess duelling by laws or are you too much of a coward to follow through with them? Referendums are a form of democracy not Geniocracy!"

I have given up on trying to manage the mood. I become angry at the insinuation that I am a coward and shout. "Of course, I have read them. You're talking rubbish. You can only challenge an individual or company representative within your own county. Why are you talking about chess when we can be taking action like the good old days?"

"I see you have only read enough to pass your exams and then have been consumed by thoughts of revolution and usurpation ever since." She has quite a nerve to speak to her boss like this, she walks over to the bookshelf and slams a hefty manual on the kitchen island. "Any council member can challenge a different county council member on matters of intra-county policy, though they may not remove or replace any individual in a county of which they are not a citizen."

"What's your point." I have folded my arms and the muscles around my mouth are in spasm.

"You convinced me to join you as your pawn because you said you were going to improve the lives of people in North Yorkshire, starting with mental health. I agreed with you when we discussed how to create a temporary economic boom with Professor Odoi. In fact, I suggested it. However, I re-emphasise, temporary economic boom! Now we are talking about secret deals made on random rowing boats where you are risking the lives and welfare of people in other counties and countries in pursuit of your own political aspirations."

"That is not true. York is North Yorkshire, through and through. I am using mental health to take back what is rightfully ours!"

"With a referendum. Yorkshire became independent because of stupid referendums. They tore the UK apart. And you want another one. Who are you? What rock have you been living under? Just challenge the East Yorkshire County Council on their policy. You realise that there are people across Yorkshire desperate for treatment whilst you are playing games. Let alone that there are still thousands in North Yorkshire who the pill has not helped. I thought we were going to use the economic boom to improve their social standards and help them, not to start insurrections in other counties territory."

"Well, you have changed your tune. Hypocrite." I say with venom.

"Why is it so surprising when someone changes their mind. I was clearly living under a delusion, that you are a nice man. Now look at you, you would fit in with the West Yorkshire bunch."

"Get out." The words escape my lips and I instantly regret them. Rosanna grabs her briefcase and flings her assortment of files into it. She leaves without a word and with her head held high. Hannah opens the door for her, and she walks through it. She's gone.

I sit down on the stool, but Hannah remains standing by the door. I put my head in my hands and embarrassingly begin to cry. I actually sob, snot and everything. It's been a stressful day.

Hannah paces around a little through the adjoining living room. Eventually she drags another stool across the floor and joins me at the kitchen island. She is a deceptively pretty woman, with striking brown eyes and long brown hair. She fidgets with her fingers and then motions with her hands to

187

indicate that she is about to speak but hesitates and stops herself. A few minutes pass before those hand gestures return, indicating she is about to speak, and she takes a leap of faith.

"I must admit, Rosanna leaving is not as big a loss as it may seem. I know you two are close, but I thought I should let you know. There is something strange about her, and don't worry I am more than capable of picking up her workload." She looks sheepish in anticipation of my reply.

I look at her in a way to encourage her to go on. It's funny how when you are annoyed with a friend all sense of loyalty flies out of the window.

"I think because you two have worked together for so long you don't have the fresh eyes that can see problems with Rosanna's work." She stops and glances at me, making sure she hasn't offended me. "She is actually quite controlling, remember, you are the councillor not her!"

She makes a fair point; I knew she could be controlling the day I met her, but I had always seen that as an advantage as it meant there would never be any indecisiveness in my office. Hannah continues, "She can be rude, superior in one moment and childish the next. Look, she is a great political advisor, no doubt about it, but she is a more low-level advisor. Now you are King's piece you need consistency not wild schemes; you need to trust yourself."

I can't shake the feeling that Hannah is just trying to capitalise on the argument Rosanna and I had just had but for now I see no harm in it.

I shake her hand. "Congratulations!" I declare, "You will be a fine King's pawn."

She smiles and looks towards the door where Rosanna had exited mere minutes ago. The body is not even cold, it was only one argument, and she has been replaced, its true what Harold Macmillan said… a week is a long time in politics.

Chapter Twenty Five: Decisions in the Dead of Night

Sometimes I am grateful that I haven't got a wife because they would never be able to cope with how little I sleep. I would drive them insane within months. Still, having someone to share all my thoughts with would be nice. Politicians throughout Yorkshire's recent history have more often than not been awful at relationships. I think of Callum, relationships are a dangerous game nowadays.

Therefore, pawns have often picked up the duty of confidant for their prospective power pieces. Losing Rosanna feels like a divorce. I am haunted by memories of our time together at every attempt to close my eyes and sleep. I find myself rolling over and checking my phone to see if she has texted. Nothing. I am half expecting her to be there when I wake up with our coffees and the latest political minefield which she thinks I should get involved in.

I chose Rosanna as my Pawn after great consideration and pleaded with her to quit her job and join me. We had met at a tennis tournament when I was 12. She was representing Skipton Grammar School for Girls; I was representing a small Christian school in Harrogate. As a teenager, I was petrified at the prospect of losing to a girl at anything, a school test, a video game or a class debate. But losing to a girl in a sporting event was the ultimate no-no. My friends would have torn me to pieces. I remember a guy I used to play football with was tackled by a girl and shoved to the floor in the process. He was known as Pathetic Pete for the rest of his school career.

Moreover, being so afraid of losing to a girl gave any female opponent an advantage, especially in tennis. I would walk out a snivelling mess and tremble at the sight of a good forehand stroke. My game with Rosanna was the exception that proved the rule. On a blustery day, autumnal leaves clattering around the concrete tennis court, I played the best tennis match of my life. I was unstoppable. I ran down every ball, hit almost every first serve in and volleyed at the opportune moments. Before every point I chuntered in my head about how I couldn't let her have a single point because that would give her the foothold to go on and win the match.

It was close but I won in 5 sets, 6-4 2-6 7-5 6-7 7-5. As we shook hands at the net she smiled and whispered, "I bet you will never be able to emulate this performance ever again." On the bus home to Harrogate my coach stood up, with the gimmick bus microphone and said we had been embarrassing to watch. "Rowan even lost two sets to a girl." Raucous laughter at my expense erupted but I wasn't fazed. This was my first realisation that sexism makes no logical sense, I knew Rosanna was a better tennis player than me. If anything, she should have won the whole tournament.

I bumped into her again and again over our high school careers. It started with tennis but then we found ourselves debating against each other for our schools, competing at maths challenges and school music concerts. She was everywhere except chess tournaments in sixth form. It was only when we had become good friends, regularly meeting up with a group at a park on Saturday nights for a drink that she told me why this was.

Her mum had written to Skipton Grammar School and said she should only be allowed to learn enough chess to pass her exams and be given no additional teaching than what was necessary. The school had refused to comply, in line with government policy. However, faced with her mum's dismay at her 'imminent death', Rosanna pledged not to try in class. She would never put herself forward for competitions or revise beyond the bear minimum. She passed, with an unremarkable score and never subjected herself to the study of chess ever again.

I lost touch with Rosanna at university. I went to York to study History whilst she went to Bradford to read law. A strange choice for someone who couldn't play much chess. Upon graduation, when considering my political future my mum suggested Rosanna as a Pawn. She was unquestionably more intelligent than me in matters of policy and legality, but more importantly, her lack of chess knowledge meant she wouldn't be a threat. In the last 40 years fifteen councillors have been executed and replaced by their pawns. It's a consideration that all prospective politicians take very seriously.

My alarm clock reads 5am when I decide to give up on sleep and try and do some work. I make myself a coffee and sit up in bed with my head resting against an upright pillow positioned against the headboard. I google 'insurrection' and give myself an overview of previous attempts across the world. I get copious useless articles about the dangers of inciting insurrection against democracy and other propaganda esq tripe. I click on the images tab and am swallowed up by an array of flags. Catalan flags, confederate flags in the Whitehouse, Yorkshire flags on Flamborough beach, the flags carry so much meaning to these people.

An hour and a half later Hannah opens the door to what must resemble a bomb site. Papers are littered across every available surface in the Octagon. I am particularly pleased with my detective style cork board with threads connecting related pinned sheets. Yorkshire flags hang from cupboards, tables, chairs and one is covering my TV set. I look at her with incredible glee and a sinister smile.

"You still have friends in the army right?" I say like a madman. I take a spray paint can and Hannah realises my plan. She takes her phone out of her pocket straight away and walks into the office to make calls. I stand back and look at my masterpiece.

"Hello York, welcome back to North Yorkshire." I deliberately shout loud enough for Hannah to hear.

Chapter Twenty Six: Influential Vandalism and other Symbolic Events

To anyone who ever reads this, this is an important day. Mark it in your textbooks. One day, today might be a bank holiday. The 20th of March 2123. At lunchtime the news was plastered wall to wall with coverage of the 'unrest' in York. Unrest is a bit of an exaggeration but with any luck we will be at that stage in a couple of weeks.

At 08:00 the East Yorkshire county council commissioned a police unit to remove graffiti on the central bridge over the river Ouse. A White Yorkshire Rose with a red 'N' was spray painted on a black wall of the pub that always floods.

At 11:27 a public announcement was delivered from the East Yorkshire First Minister, Jonathan Hyde, to discourage the 'inflammatory' and 'reckless' spray painting of White Roses with Red Ns across the city of York. I watch on with devilish admiration of Hannah's work.

By 17:00 our variant North Yorkshire flag was all that could be seen in York city centre. Some innovative protesters had even defaced the natural roses in the flower beds surrounding the castle with red food colouring N shapes, distorted by the lay of each flower's petals.

Hannah and I are at a standing table at a local bar. I couldn't be in the Octagon without Rosanna for a moment like this, but I still wanted to celebrate. This pub is unique in that it is incredibly grand but does not house a fancy clientele. A broad circular staircase with golden handrails proudly stands in the middle of the pub and yet the people are in tracksuits and hoodies. It is truly a pub of the people, no less than what the people of Yorkshire deserve. Surrounded by wealth yet expressing our individuality. What a place to celebrate.

Hannah is minorly inebriated by now and is mouthing off about her friends. "I feel like a master choreographer!" She says drunkenly with a waft of bad breath coming my way. I recoil at her breath but sympathise with her feelings. All we did was put up one rose symbol and the people have responded. I feel vindicated since the people of York obviously want to be part of North Yorkshire, all they needed was a push to let their voices be heard.

We are celebrating but we are also acutely aware that this may be premature. History has proven time and time again that the voices that are loud are not always the majority. There may only be a few people involved with all the roses in York today, we need to analyse the strength of feeling and consolidate the argument in the average person's mind.

Most of the patrons of the pub are watching the football. Sheffield United vs Leeds United has become a major event in the Yorkshire calendar year and the tension is electrifying. You could hear a pin drop one moment and the next you can't hear the person stood next to you. Hannah and I begin to discuss phase two of the plan.

"We need to implant the idea of a referendum." Hannah suggests.

"Yes, but we must be so careful! We cannot afford to let anyone know that we are in on this. It must be seen as spontaneous, the unadulterated will of the people." I am still fairly sober so speak without the characteristic drunken voice.

"Actually, scrap that! I think the best idea, is to wait for the East Yorkshire Council to make a mistake. Let's sit on the idea until we can publicly denounce something that the East Yorkshire Council do. We have a small amount of time. They will try to prevent protests or arrest someone. As soon as they do, we strike."

Hannah is not paying attention. She is glancing over my shoulder towards the bar every few seconds and looking increasingly uncomfortable with every glance. I begin to turn my head to see what the matter is, but she grasps my hand giving me the signal to stop.

She whispers now, so quietly that I have to lean in. We must look like school children having a secret gossip at lunchtime. "The lighting is quite dim so I cannot be sure, but I think we have been recognised."

I raise a quizzical eyebrow, "Why is that a problem?"

"I think we have been recognised by someone who is not a huge fan of yours." She hisses. "I saw him ten minutes or so ago looking at us and chatting with someone. He left and has now come back alone with a brown paper bag."

"You're sounding a little paranoid, are you sure you've only been drinking?" I joke to try and lighten the mood, but she is deathly serious. I am intrigued as to how fast she has sobered up. She must have some special ability.

"He is walking this way, averting his gaze. We need to move. Slowly but decisively get your coat and let's go." She says more like a secret agent than a former veteran. As I turn to put my arms in the sleeves of my jacket I see the figure she is referring to. He is a larger man, probably with a BMI over 30. He has a scraggly beard and is wearing an ill-fitting tracksuit jacket with Harrogate Town FC emblazoned on it. He weaves through the football fans at their round tables with ease for such a large man.

I hasten my exit but cannot get my zip to work. Hannah takes my arm and begins to drag me towards the courtyard exit, whilst I continue to fumble with my jacket. We are within touching distance of the large patio window leading into the night air when I feel the horrible sensation of viscous liquid moving down my back. I jerk my head back in response which was a huge mistake as a second wave of fluid drenches my face from behind.

The people around us at the back of the pub gasp in horror. I hear murmurs of "That's Schofield!" and "Should we call someone?" but nothing happens. Everyone goes silent. Well, almost everyone, the hardcore football fans do not move an inch. I cannot see anything as I am afraid to open my eyes in case the fluid will hurt them. I stumble about and walk into a table.

I feel a hand take mine and a stranger say, "Here you go!" I grasp some tissue paper in my hand, napkins I presume and use it to dab my eyes. As soon as I feel comfortable enough to open my eyes I see the cause of the problem. I am looking down at a table with droplets of red paint erratically marking the sticky pub table. The poor couple enjoying their drinks have moved their pint glasses to the opposite end of the table and are looking at me with a mixture of sympathy and apprehension.

"Thank you so much!" I say as kindly and politely as I can because I am aware many people are watching and this will almost certainly make the news. Thank goodness the coverage of York will put it down the headline list though. I vaguely hear Hannah berating someone and turn to see the carnage behind me.

Red paint is splattered all over the floor and a few tables. Some drinkers are screaming about the state of their clothes and Hannah is rebuking a lanky security guard for his lack of awareness, "What if he had had a gun!" Amidst it all is the overweight man whose eyes remain fixed on me.

He is not responding to the howls of the collateral damage and actually looks quite moved with emotion. From his right hand an empty paint tin dangles and bits of paint are visible on his fingers. It makes me think of the phrase *caught red handed*.

I take a step towards him and he flinches. He mumbles something but I can't make out what he is saying. I raise my palm towards the crowd and hushes ring out. Even the football hooligans are taking a break from the game to listen in. I nod enthusiastically to indicate that the floor is his.

"I am sorry, but I had to." He says a little pathetically and the crowd scoffs.

"Why did you have to?" I say with a booming voice as a hint to the crowd to be quiet. I must look ridiculous.

"The Schofield pill is a lie." He says but looks at the floor. "Your people promised me your pill would change my life. They promised me. Politicians all promise but it's just self-serving lies. My life is just as awful as it has always been! I am out of work, once again. If no one will employ me when the going is good, what hope do I have for a stable job in the bad times!"

"What do you normally work as?" I ask with an empathetic tone, but I am enraged inside.

"I'm a carpenter. I had a rough spell last year when my wife died and was let go for taking too many sick days. The doctor gave me some tablets that made me feel drowsy, but they made me feel worse. I applied for mental health disability, they said I was unemployed before the law change so I couldn't get help. They brought out a pill for depression. I begged my doctor. I begged her! She finally got it for me but now look at me, destitute as normal."

"So why did you put paint on me?" Two female police officers have arrived, but they are letting me finish talking to the man before they intervene.

"To show the world that you are not a miracle worker. You're just like us, a liar with some skills. This pill helps some people, but the people like me just feel more hopeless. We cannot get help anymore. People don't think we are really depressed if this treatment doesn't work. Trust me, suicide rates are gonna go up." The man is in tears, I feel sympathetic but also annoyed at the way this man has gone about making his point.

The police take the momentary lull as the opportunity to arrest the man. He looks downtrodden as they read him his memoranda rights and place him against the wall. I feel huge pressure to say something in response to the concerns he has raised and think back to the banners on Knaresborough Castle by the river.

There is a captive audience here and no politician worth their salt could resist. I wave my hands in the air and shout, "I recognise things are not perfect with mental health yet. I know there have been wild claims about NSSRIs being a cure. Let me dispel that rumour. We have always known the pills would only help some, I am surprised at how effective it has been! That does not, for one moment, mean that others suffering with mental illness which has not improved on NSSRIs are lying or have been misdiagnosed. All it means, is that they need a different type of treatment. I promise we will not rest until we have found further solutions."

My speech is cut short by the arrested man, squished up against the wall, finally finding his voice. "Is that another promise I hear?" he wails sarcastically. The crowd murmur and dissipate before I can rebuttal. Opportunity lost.

Chapter Twenty Seven: Radio Interviews – To Referendum or not to Referendum

Some new politicians are absolutely clueless. Low and behold the white square knight of East Yorkshire, some idiot named Colin Trek, called the protesters "mentally ill lunatics" last night and now we are set to pounce. The protests have progressed from spray paint to acts of defiance. My personal favourite from Amanda Buckle's summary this morning was a little boy who had drawn a chalk line, at the direction of his father, around where he thought the new North Yorkshire border should lie. This chalk line now runs 12 miles, due the assistance of many other schoolchildren. Some schools cancelled lessons to take their classes out to the 'new border' and help with the chalk line.

Hannah has organised an interview with a Radio station in York this morning. I love doing radio interviews! No makeup, no body language and you can make all the faces you want. There are some caveats however, you have to be extremely conscious of your tone of voice and if possible add some additional gravitas. It would also be fair to say that many radio interviewers are better skilled than the pretty boy TV presenters and can grill you ferociously. I remember one lady who deliberately positioned my microphone too high so that I felt like I was constantly straining, just to put me on edge for the interview.

I am sat in a dingy recording studio with a plastic cup, half filled with water, on the table in front of me. There is a young man hosting the radio show today. He looks like he's in his 20s and has thickly gelled hair making him look as though he should be on a game show. It's strange to see someone, whose profession is to be heard and not seen, looking so dapper. He introduces me as, "the man causing so many of us to question our county's identity." Quite a flattering line to introduce a politician I must say.

"Tell us councillor Schofield, before we get ahead of ourselves, would North Yorkshire even want us back?" He asks in a friendly and affirming manner.

"Well, that question is easy to answer! York should always have been in North Yorkshire; you guys were cruelly taken away from us! We would accept York back in a heartbeat, but only if that is the will of the people." My answer has drawn a smile from the fresh-faced interviewer.

Hannah advised me to be inflammatory in this interview and I agree that it is the right tact. We need as many citizens to listen as possible; it doesn't matter if they agree or disagree right now. We need to start the conversation in every house, every workplace and on every street corner. We need the discussion to dominate every area of life until a referendum is inevitable. The radio show presenter seems to have cottoned on to the views he is going to get online after this.

"Let me ask you about the benefits of being a North Yorkshire citizen. We have heard a lot in recent days about the state support offered by East Yorkshire, the interconnections with the major fishing port in Grimsby and York's investment programme in the arts. These arguments have swayed a lot of people in favour of remaining in East Yorkshire. What do you have to say in favour of North Yorkshire?" You can tell this chap has been practising that question in the shower.

"Let me start by re-iterating, I am not trying to start any problems. I have been invited by yourself and your team of your own volition, is that not correct?"

"Absolutely!"

"OK. Well, let us examine some of those claims. East Yorkshire does have a strong state support system. North Yorkshire a smaller package of state intervention but we can do that because we have higher rates of employment and let us not forget, medical interventions that no other county can compete with."

"So, what you're saying is that North Yorkshire citizens require less state support." He summarises.

"Precisely! We do have impoverished people and homelessness. Of course, we do. But we have communities of high employment, good mental health and high-quality education. We invested in the people, not the state, and we have come out on top. Now we can focus our state intervention on those who need it most." I am pleased with my response and, because we are on the radio, I can show it.

"Those other points are neither here nor there. What does York care about a fishing port! North Yorkshire has Whitby, the fish and chips are just as good." We both have a little chuckle. "Listen, the reasons for being a North Yorkshire citizen are obvious. We are all Yorkshire through and through no matter which county we live in, just some of our views are different. We believe York is a beacon of hope and the Jewell in the crown of North Yorkshire. East Yorkshire believe York is a cash-cow and should be in submission to their monstrous state machine." The poor interviewer is struggling to decipher between my nice tone and conciliatory language and the occasional deliberate interjection of extremely inflammatory content.

"You know what councillor. I actually understand what you're saying." I am quite taken aback; the guy is breaking his non-bias clause. I didn't see this coming. "I have been working here for three years now and I have already been receiving messages about what is illegal to talk about now compared to when I started. That's not freedom! Did you know, I am not allowed to mention the Schofield pill? In an interview with Rowan Schofield! What happened to freedom of the press? It's like we are living in the UK again."

The guy is breaking down in front of my eyes. He is on the verge of a tirade. I stretch my arm over the table, through a mesh of wires and grasp his forearm. "Not long till you are free again." I say this quietly but loud enough that the microphones can still pick it up.

Hannah meets me in the lobby with a grin from ear to ear. She is standing bolt upright, like the true soldier she is, but her phone is buzzing like crazy which makes her look bizarre. Like she has a neurological disease affecting only one leg. She tries to conceal the buzzing my placing pressure on her pocket subtly, but it just makes the sight even funnier.

"I have two pieces of good news for you!" She says, beaming with pride. "Firstly, you smashed it in there and we have to leave York with a guarded escort because so many people want to see you!"

"Haha, finally I have achieved celebrity status." I joke.

"Secondly, the man with the paint." I raise my eyebrows, intrigued about his fate. "Sentenced to a year in minimum security prison for disturbing the peace."

"That's a little harsh don't you think?" I ask with genuine compassion. The guy was an inconvenience, but I understand where he was coming from. "His life sounded terrible as it is! A prison sentence will end any prospect of him finding work."

"In the grand scheme of things boss, he is small fry. However, if what happened in the pub had been filmed he could have been a serious

209

problem! Now, anyone who hears the story of the paint and the pub will also hear that he is in prison. That puts the things he rightfully said in a whole different perspective… We win." Hannah comes across cold and callous.

All is fair in love and warfare. And hopefully we will win York back in the process. The means justify the ends. This is right. I am sure of it. Completely sure.

Chapter Twenty Eight: Geniocracy in practice

Geniocracy was never intended to completely replace democracy. Or, at least, that is what I have been saying hundreds of times over this past week. Referendums are one of the nightmares in democracy that caused the collapse of the UK. I want to cause a collapse of the current county system. So, I want a referendum. East Yorkshire county councillors want to settle this with geniocracy based challenges. They have been saying the people of York are welcome to challenge councillors and create a policy change through the established system. Too slow, Katherine will make the deal in less than two months now. East Yorkshire just have to hold out.

I call Katherine who assures me she will not even hint to the East Yorkshire delegates that there is a deal on the horizon. Any indication may change the way they play the political game over the next month or so. She seems optimistic about my progress although she doesn't show any signs of extending our agreed upon time frame.

I miss Rosanna bitterly. Hannah is a great person and good at her job but, through no fault of her own, she just isn't as fun as Rosanna. She doesn't push me like Rosanna did. I don't feel like I am at the top of my game. I just don't feel right. I have tried to send her a message, but I end up typing out mean comments and angry sentences. So, I gave up. Knowing Rosanna, she has already found another job somewhere. She always said she would have liked to have been a journalist, but I was worried she would end up advising another councillor if I ever let her go. I've asked around quietly, she hasn't reared her head yet. I need to get her back.

I write an email in the few minutes I have before I need to leave for a council meeting.

Dear Rosanna,

I was hasty in what I said before and want to discuss our ideas properly. We have always been a good team, and I need you back on my side before York goes to pot. Call me when you get a chance.

Rowan

It is cringey but I send it anyway. I don't have the time to craft a speech and Rosanna would see through that anyway.

The council meeting is predictable. Katherine and I discussing complicated political matters, the rest of the council cowering behind their pretend concern about when we will release the NSSRIs to the rest of Yorkshire. The Leeds born, new council member will never let the topic go whilst Anthony rocks back and forth in this chair, assessing which side he will be on at the next turning point in history. I have concerns he has been having secret meetings with West Yorkshire Officials. Katherine never says anything, but she has some secret service members loyal to her and I am sure they are keeping her in the loop about all of our activities.

As we leave the giant meeting hall and cross the expansive corridor, I notice Katherine walking close behind me, eyes fixed on the decorative carpet beneath our feet. She murmurs, "Hang back…" and I do as I am told in a manner as secretive as I can muster. Maybe I should have been in the secret service, but that would have been a waste of my love of public speaking. By the time the other councillors and their respective pawns have filed out into the journalist saturated courtyard Katherine has ushered me into a small interview room.

The room is baffling. It seems like such a waste of space. It is no larger than a walk-in wardrobe and contains three wooden chairs. Bright green cushions make the room even more unappealing, and I wonder whether this is the first time this room has been used since the revolution itself. We find ourselves in an interview like arrangement of seating when Michael, Katherine's pawn, enters and assumes the chair next to Katherine. Interview has turned to interrogation.

"What happened to Rosanna?" Katherine speaks with her classic bluntness, but I have not seen this from her since I got into her good books.

"She quit, we disagreed about our little arrangement. She is of a similar mind set to the rest of our pathetic council."

"She is a formidable asset that you should not have let go. You will regret not patching up your differences." Katherine is looking at me the way a professor would look over glasses poised on the tip of their nose.

"Hannah is more than capable of wearing Rosanna's shoes." I reply stoically, unmoved at this attempt to demean me.

"Say it ten more times and I might believe you." Katherine retorts.

"Moving on." Michael says, always professional and looking to get his boss to the next important engagement. "East Yorkshire have asked to have a representative duel to settle the York debacle."

"What on earth is that? Just hold out for a referendum. We are on the cusp of reclaiming our land without a single death."

"You know what they said about referendums in the former UK?" Katherine says with unbearable intensity and not wanting me to attempt any reply. "That they cause irreparable division. You know how long it took to recover from the Brexit referendum? Or how about the Scottish Independence referendum? They needed three of them before Scotland went independent and low and behold here we sit in an independent Yorkshire. Referendums ruin countries."

I move in my chair to begin my reply, but Katherine intercepts my retort. "I will not have Yorkshire collapse on my watch." She is stern, no other word for it.

Michael comes to my aid. "Here is the proposal." He says with kindness as he passes me a dossier. It reads:

The people's representatives for East Yorkshire request the attendance of five North Yorkshire Council Officials to compete to decide the future of York. In light of recent events, public opinion in York is increasingly divided on the issue. We would like to avoid any civil unrest, after all, we have learnt from the lessons the revolution provided us.

The proposed tournament would consist of five chess matches. The county which wins three or more chess matches will have ten days to propose a solution to the people of York. There will then be a fortnight cooling off period where any protests from the people of York can be assessed and each individual citizen will be provided with the opportunity to challenge the legislation and any prospective councillors on the victor's county council. Provided there are no major developments in this process the legislation will be passed and both sides will agree to uphold this ruling indefinitely.

216

I look forward to your response,

Yours sincerely,

Jonathan Hyde

This declaration of interest is followed by a series of documents outlining the rules of the chess challenge. I am stuck by how reasonable the proposal is but feel a deep stubbornness rising from within me.

"This is a well worded surrender document. Why would we engage?" The stubbornness has broken forth.

"I feared you would say something like that." Say Katherine. "People are starting to say you are acting like a coward. Your elevated status in the public eye means you haven't faced a challenge in roughly two months right?"

"Right."

"So, are you trying to start a potentially devastating referendum to avoid getting what you want at the chess board? We live in a geniocracy and the talk-show stuff about never meaning to replace democracy completely doesn't fly with us." She shuffles in her seat.

"I don't quite understand what I have done to offend you, Katherine. I seem to remember you sharing a similar dislike of West Yorkshire. Whatever the cause of your change of heart, I deserve to be treated with a modicum of respect given what I have achieved."

"Your ego is inflating, young man. You sound like a challenger you once faced, like a teenager who thinks they are the future of the world." I remember that kid and realise Katherine is actually talking some sense to me. As much as it pains me to hear such accurate criticism, the marker of success is how you take criticism, not how much praise you receive.

"Who do you have in mind to play on our behalf?" I ask, trying to distract from the fact that I am compromising on my outburst of philosophical passion.

"We need five members of the council. The best chess players may not be the best choices. Those Leeds born weasels may lose on purpose so that discounts James and Vanessa. In reality we only need three strong players. Anthony, despite being a painfully difficult person, is an excellent chess player. Why do you think he has lasted so long?"

"We would have to offer him an incentive to perform!" I say after a moment's hesitation. I hate Anthony.

"I have just the thing in mind. I take it you agree to the challenge?" She stands up and Michael closes his laptop lid.

"Yes First Minister. Although, I would request that we choose which players play whom. That gives us some control over where to position our best players."

"I think we can negotiate that; glad you're seeing sense." She leaves with a slam of the door. I feel a bit betrayed and hurt from the discussion. Fair though it was, getting brought back down to Earth is never a pleasant experience.

Hannah and I ride back to the Octagon in silence.

Chapter Twenty Nine: Jorvik

There is a famous museum in York. The Jorvik Viking Centre. It is inspired by the true story of the invasion of the UK by Vikings. I am hoping to use some Viking strength to get through this week. The situation with my brother has calmed down and he is on the mend meaning I am able to devote all of my attention to the duelling competition.

{Kaley Abrahams: On consultation with North Yorkshire County Council's administration department, I discovered some sections from this account were removed as they were deemed private in nature. From context I believe one of Mr Schofield's brothers, most likely Kalvin, required a brief hospital admission. Kalvin died two years later from cardiovascular disease which is why this seems to be the most likely explanation.}

Katherine managed to convince Anthony to duel. She has declined to inform me of the exact details of their little arrangement, but I have a feeling it relates to who will be overseeing, and therefore getting the credit for, the transition of York back into North Yorkshire. On review of the other council members, we went with one of the newbies named Sophie Cole and the longest serving council member, Beth Ingram. Sorry for the recap, I feel this may be necessary given the Hodge podge of poor accounts I've written over the last week due to all the stress. I recognise that it is my legal duty to provide an accurate account of events and so I am attempting to fulfil that requirement here to the best of my ability.

I swear that I do not know the exact details of Katherine's deal with Anthony. I know that's what lots of politicians say but I honestly do not. I had bigger fish to fry this week.

Thankfully Katherine has been quite accommodating of my personal issues and has made herself available for phone calls. I gave her permission to use Hannah whilst I was away and Hannah has given me regular updates. East Yorkshire accepted our demand that we decide who plays whom after some resistance since they had originally planned that power pieces would play their opposite numbers. The itinerary that they eventually decided upon is as follows:

1. Katherine Tyne (Queen's piece NY) vs Jonathan Hyde (Queen's piece EY)

2. Rowan Schofield (King's piece NY) vs Muhammed Abel (Black Square Bishop EY)
3. Anthony Peal (White Square Bishop NY) vs Ayesha Redmain (White Square Bishop EY)
4. Beth Ingram (White Square Rook NY) vs Rhys Davidson (Queen's piece EY)
5. Sophie Cole (Black Square Knight NY) vs Alexis Otoje (White Square Rook EY)

Katherine and Jonathan basically had to face each other. The press frenzy after the tournament was announced essentially demanded that the pair faced each other. Katherine could not arrange to face someone else for fear of being deemed a coward by the public. Whoever wins that match will make the headlines and it is extremely important that we win. However, all that matters is that we win three games, we can afford to lose two. Anthony and I should win, although I offered to face Muhammed as he is better than Sophie and Beth and we couldn't risk a guaranteed loss.

I am struggling to hype myself up tonight. I am sat over a chess board with a book on chess openings in my left hand. Hannah is on her computer in the living room watching videos of Muhammed's previous games. Poor woman, she must have watched all his games hundreds of times over this week, she is nervous on my behalf.

"Hannah, I know you have never been in a chess duel but going into it without any fear of death is making me feel like I am not on top of my game."

"I've never been in a duel, but I have been in the army." She palms me off.

"Good point, so how did you hype yourself up for training exercises?" I ask.

"I realised that training exercises prepared me for real life consequences." She hasn't looked up from her computer once. "Your consequences include losing York, losing your political credibility and in case you haven't figured it out yet; if you lose you are sure to be challenged by members of the public."

My fear levels have gone from zero to off the charts in the moments Hannah has been talking. I return my gaze to the chess board and my concentration levels are heightened like a normal duel once more. I wish Rosanna was about nonetheless, she would have hyped me up without making me think I was going to lose.

We leave at 6:30am and arrive in York by 7am. York Minster is, I must say, the best place for a chess duel. I feel like royalty as I enter. I have a police escort through adoring fans and irritating journalists. The Minster is the pinnacle of Yorkshire's historic pride, it is fitting that we are here to decide York's future. The gothic architecture looks out across the entire city and, to my delight, on entry there is a giant flag with a Yorkshire rose on it. Some loyal supporters have managed to sneak into the minster and paint a red N through it.

I spot the Archbishop looking up at the flag. The Minster is quiet inside, with security ensuring our privacy before the cameras turn on. I meander up to the Most Reverend Archbishop Sentamu and stand beside him, joining his gaze.

"My great grandfather was the Archbishop of York when it was still part of the UK." Says the Reverend. We do not look at each other. "I wonder what he would have made of an occasion like today?"

"I could not possibly speak on behalf of someone as amazing as your grandfather." I reply with an attempt at humility. "But I hope he would have simply prayed that God's will be done."

"Spoken like a man who believes they are doing the work of God." Archbishop Sentamu is archbishop for a reason I conclude. "Just be careful. Whatever happens, God works all things together for the good of those who love him. East Yorkshire or North Yorkshire, God will always be present." With that he walks away into the crypt and is gone.

The set up for the tournament is strikingly familiar. Standard rules apply, of course the forfeit has been removed. Each player will have 90 minutes each on their clocks. All matches will be played today starting with Match 5 and finishing with Katherine and Jonathan. The aim is to have taken the victory by mid-afternoon to remove all the pressure from Katherine. I am scheduled to play at 1:30pm.

A blonde girl, who must have been on her summer holidays, dressed in a red velvet waistcoat and white shirt rushes up to me and breathlessly informs me that I have to move right this instant before they let members of the public in, "to ensure my safety." I take her cue, although I do not believe for one second that I need protecting and am ushered into a side room with refreshments and an array of TV screens.

"You will be able to view the matches from in here. If you wish to see the matches in person this can be arranged, just ring the buzzer and inform the staff so they can attach a security detail to your side."

I smile and ask, "Will the other council members be joining me in here?"

"Yes, sir. They should be arriving soon." She curtseys and leaves through the giant oak door in a hurry. I haven't seen someone curtsey in a long time.

Chapter Thirty: Game, Set, Match

"This is a bad idea. So many high-profile politicians in one room. On a contested border. We are sitting ducks." Anthony is pacing up and down our stone-paved side room.

"Sit down you utter lunatic. No one is going to blow us up. This isn't a spy novel." Beth Ingram is one of the most straight forward people I have ever met. Her parents were doctors who moved here from Nigeria. She inherited her mother's surgeon consultation style, straight to the point and then move on. Her Father is a psychiatrist. I would have loved to be a fly on the wall in their house when she was younger.

Sophie is about halfway through the opening match and is doing terribly. She lost her rook in a stupid sequence and now has her queen pinned into a corner. They have only been playing for half an hour as well. Thankfully the atmosphere in our little room is quite calm. Katherine is not arriving until later as she has some meetings apparently, so the pressure doesn't feel overwhelming.

Sophie made a minor recovery, took two pawns without response, but she didn't sort out her defensive mess and returned to our hovel embarrassed. We did our best to reassure her, but we didn't really care. We are all too focussed on our own games.

Councillor Ingram is next, and she is a formidable chess player. With a win from her we are back on level terms and should pinch glory.

The opening by Beth is textbook but sadly so is the response by Rhys. One of the drawbacks of being a councillor for so long is that there are so many previous games for opponents to watch and try to use against you. The Queen's Gambit has been declined by Rhys (an annoying variation where there are far too many pawns in the middle of the board). One of the advantages of being a councillor for so long is that Beth has a proven innate chess ability that is a rare talent. She has seen of so many challengers that people have given up. She hasn't been challenged in well over a year. Hannah, Katherine and I had worried this would mean she would be rusty, but she is showing no signs of that.

Beth won in just over an hour and a quarter. It was quite a competitive match to be fair to Rhys and he should be proud of his performance against such

an accomplished and long-standing chess expert.
Beth walks into our little room, sits down, gets out
her book and reads like nothing has happened. I
look at her with quiet admiration, Anthony looks at
her with loud exasperation.

"Good job." Say Anthony, a little jealously actually
which makes me question his chess ability. Does
he think he would lose to Beth? It is 11:00 and
since Beth and Sophie were so quick we have an
hour break.

The TV cuts straight to 'In-depth' analysis which is
about as in-depth as the shallow end of a toddler's
swimming pool. The interesting segment of the
news reporting for us is the response to the events
from York citizens. We have one television set
tuned to Amanda Buckle and one to some East
Yorkshire news anchor. It is frankly astounding
how different their reports are. Amanda seems to
have found overwhelming support for the North
whilst this East Yorkshire bloke has nothing but
East Yorkshire supporters on his show. Sophie
and I look at each other and nod knowingly.

"Journalists…" says Sophie and then goes to the
refreshment table.

Amidst the low-level murmurs of the four of us
councillors talking business with our pawns who

were allowed to enter during the break, Katherine arrives with Michael in tow. She looks a little unwell if I am being honest. Pale. She takes a seat in the far corner of the room and sips on a drink Michael gets for her.

I can't take my eyes off her. It is interesting watching all these seasoned professionals preparing for duels in their own style. Anthony has also gone quiet, and his pawn has taken a deliberate step away from him. Clearly this is the normal process for them. The hour flies by and before I know it the pawns are being asked to leave. I don't really understand why they can't stay but the blonde girl assures me the East Yorkshire officials are not allowed their pawns either.

Katherine stands up and pats Anthony of the back. "Knock em dead." She says and he exists hesitantly.

He looks conflicted on camera when he sits down. Beth was white for the previous game and so Anthony is playing black. This takes the initiative away from him as he basically just has to respond to whatever Ayesha starts with. So why is he looking so conflicted?

The atmosphere in our little cupboard of a room has changed with the arrival of Katherine. Sophie seems to be in awe of Katherine and approaches her like a fan girl running into their hero at an airport. Beth couldn't care less and continues to read her book. Katherine comes and sits next to me; I think mainly just to get a better view of the TV.

"This should be an easy win and then it's just down to you." She mutters.

"Something doesn't feel right to me."

"Trust me, he has enough incentive to play properly." Katherine says with extreme confidence.

It is evident that Ayesha Redmain has done her homework and I am surprised that she has not crossed my radar before, after seeing her play a variant called the centre game with great competence. She looks like a kindly woman. She has dark brown hair and large framed glasses giving her a studious look, she has acne scars all over her face. An hour in and Anthony and Ayesha are equal in pieces taken and have a fairly even position on the board.

The TV commentators have gone quiet as the length of each turn begins to stretch towards the five-minute mark. Katherine and I watch in tense silence. Sophie watches Katherine and Beth couldn't care less. I get a sense that Katherine is getting restless. She moves her legs and then folds her arms.

"Why hasn't he taken the pawn?" She leans over and asks me.

It takes me quite some time to spot what she is talking about. I have been thinking about my own match to be frank. On closer inspection it becomes obvious that Anthony has a free pawn, a pawn he can take without any loss of a piece in return. It is quite an obvious move, even to a beginner. Eventually the commentator uses an arrow to indicate that this is the most obvious move next, maybe some viewers were getting bored.

With disbelief Katherine and I watch Anthony grasp his King and castle into the left-hand corner. It is a genuinely stupid move. Castling is a good idea early on in a match or if there is substantial pressure on the king's position. But the way Anthony has used this move now, he may as well have forfeited his move. The TV commentators have gone wild. They are talking about how, under the pressure of the game, obvious moves can be missed. Katherine and I suspect something more sinister is going on.

Ayesha is also taken aback. A wave of relief is visible on her face and she pushes the same pawn forward into a suddenly threatening position. Beth looks up from her book and takes a moment to convey her dismay in a look towards me.

"Looks like you both have to win now." Beth says and returns to her book without any further display of emotion.

Under the cosh now Anthony plays out the game with just enough effort to fool the untrained eye into thinking he had been bested by Ayesha. Katherine and I know better. Ayesha claims the victory with apparent surprise. Katherine gets up and kicks her chair towards the wall. Sophie looks on like a deer in headlights.

Anthony does not return to our room. The camera crews follow him into a black car which departs in the direction of Harrogate.

"Whatever you used to incentivise him wasn't enough." I say with genuine anger. "But we have to move on and move on quick."

Katherine is looking at the grey slate walls in her little corner of the room. "We must not lose this tournament. I mean it. It would be political ruin.

Everything we have achieved; we will only be remembered for losing in York Minster."

"Katherine, don't you see. If we lose, we will be challenged back home hundreds of times over. We won't survive the month with our lives."

"Go out and win Rowan. Take no prisoners. Have no fun for the cameras. Don't say a word. Just ruin Muhammed at the chess board."

Chapter Thirty One:
Playing Under Pressure

I am more afraid of what will happen than I have ever been before in a chess match. I am not going to be killed if I lose today, I try to remind myself. Just everything that means anything to me will have been ruined. My legacy will be destroyed, and I will probably be killed in a matter of weeks by an angry challenger who thinks I am incompetent.

Muhammed is awaiting me at the table. I have the privilege of playing White, a minor advantage but one I have every intention of exploiting. Muhammed is a lovely man, and he stands for me when I arrive, to shake hands. A classy move and the first person to do such a thing at this tournament. I take it warmly but remind myself that I must not get distracted from the matter at hand.

I play a classic king's pawn opening and establish my familiar set up. Muhammed seems pleased I am playing like I normally do and performs the correct counter position. This is exactly what I want him to do. It is a risky idea but having reflected on it late last night I think my best bet at a swift victory. Simply put, I want to lull him into a false sense of security.

It is often noted that when a chess match, or any event, is going exactly as planned, a sudden deviation from the plan can throw the opponent. Even if they recover initially, the sudden change will remove their confidence and lead to mistakes. Muhammed is a good player, I am playing him instead of the others for a reason, I need to encourage the mistake.

A thought runs across my mind. Why didn't we get Beth to play Muhammed? But I try to throw this out of my head. Not helpful right now.

We have arrived at the moment I had planned to shake things up. We have been playing for less time than I would have liked before invoking my game changing move. I wanted to give him more time to settle in. Now comes the difficult part. I have to take a long time, a very long time, before making a move I already know I am going to make. I have to temporarily become an actor, look like I am deep in thought, analysing a board that I have already analysed hundreds of times over in the last few days.

I let the time pass. It is actually quite boring. Like waiting for someone to play their scrabble move when you know it won't affect where you are going to play. I can imagine the atmosphere in our broom closet room, Katherine may be worried I am pulling an Anthony whilst the TV commentators have probably got their arrows out to show where most people would play in this position.

After fifteen painful minutes of pretend studying. I play the wayward move that looks bizarre. I move my queen one square forward. Innocuous. In fact, it quite literally changes nothing. But when an opponent moves a queen, alarm bells ring and they ring very loud. Muhammed's move, if he continues the standard set up, would place him in a strong position. However, he looks confused. Thank goodness.

Minutes go by. He is scanning all the possible options. He thinks I have seen something he has missed. Despite all his knowledge, years of experience and extensive reading he thinks I have somehow developed a new scheme that will ruin the classic King's pawns defence. Fear is a strange thing. All he has to do is trust his knowledge and he will have the upper hand.

We pass the 20-minute mark on his turn. One turn is taking up twenty minutes! I realise I need to play along to ensure he makes the mistake though. I show how restless I am for him to make a move by gently tapping my foot against the floor. I can only do this for a minute or so before a man in a red velvet waistcoat and who spends a lot of time in the gym asks me to stop. We are playing between the choir stalls to allow some people to sit and watch but also to give the camera crews easy set-up. There are a few lucky members of the public in the stalls watching with eager anticipation. There are candles illuminating the beautiful hall and I am admiring the stone pillars when Muhammed finally makes his move.

He moves his knight into a position to block my Queen's route to his back line. He has taken the bait. We are in unknown territory now, and that is where I thrive. We have both lost a lot of time on our clocks and so the moves will also be fast, increasingly the chances of additional mistakes.

The pace picks up dramatically and it isn't long before I have managed to gain a bishop in return for a pawn, two points to the good. With Muhammed lacking a power piece, I am able to manipulate the board into a closed position. Muhammed has resorted to depending on knights to block advances towards a checkmate.

I manage to force a trade of queens. When you are winning, trading pieces keeps you in the lead and reduces your opponent's fire power. Without queens we enter a complicated and intense close quarters match. I push my advantage and manage to secure a few more pawns. Both of our clocks are now reading less than ten minutes with Muhammed having slightly less time due to that long turn he took.

It seems crazy that only half an hour ago I was looking around the Minster in boredom and now I am so concentrated on the board I can hardly hear myself think. Thankfully, Muhammed has less time than me and he is feeling the time pressure. He moves his king to hide it behind a pawn barrier. This move shows the time pressure he is feeling. Although it looks more protected, there is a clear progression with my knights to force a checkmate. I have an extra minute and use the additional seconds to triple check that my sequence works.

3 minutes left.

I feel confident enough and push my knight forward, putting my plan into motion. He replies incredibly quickly, his time is so short. He is following the defensive pattern I was expecting him to follow, it must have dawned on him that moving his king was a problem.

He pre-empts the inevitable checkmate.

He knocks his King over and it bounces against the board. Resignation.

He stands to shake my hand. I take it gratefully. I've done my part. Now it's down to Katherine.

North Yorkshire 2: East Yorkshire 2

Chapter Thirty Two: First Ministers

On arrival back in our room, even I chuckle at the News presenters' word play: Now for the battle of the Ministers in York Minster. Aside from the TV, there isn't a sound in the room. The tension is awful. I have just won a difficult duel, the hardest match I have possibly ever played and yet I am unable to celebrate. All our hopes rest on Katherine. I have a sudden realisation of how noble she is, she pushed for this tournament to take place, knowing it could potentially be the end of her long and prestigious career as First Minister. Her legacy and reputation may well rise or fall depending on the next three hours or so.

She is sat in her corner of the room again with Michael by her side. They are actually sat in what looks like quite a comfortable silence although she is a little paler than before. She gives me a thumbs up as I walk to the refreshment table. I hope I didn't add to her stress with my unusual game plan. Must have been uncomfortable viewing.

Watching the TV coverage reminds me that the blonde girl offered me the opportunity to sit in the choir stalls and watch the chess match directly. I bump into Hannah who rushes through the Oak door to congratulate me.

"Well done!" She exclaims.

"No time, ask that blonde usher if I can have an escort to the choir stands." Hannah exits as quickly as she came in.

As Katherine gets ready to leave, Beth stands and begins to clap. In seconds we have formed a guard on honour for Katherine who leaves the room to great cheers and applause. She deserves it. She is the reason we have got this far. From the beginning she backed my hairbrained ideas. She is the reason that the mental health legislation passed. She is the reason we are in York Minster. It is fitting that she is the one to win the victory for North Yorkshire and for the people of York. I hope.

As we watch Katherine take her seat, Jonathan is yet to emerge on the scene, a muscular woman enters and marches towards my seat. She is Latino and speaks with an East Yorkshire accent. She is wearing all black with a bullet proof vest that reads 'Security' across the front. She salutes and stands rigidly in front of me, I almost want to say, 'at ease soldier.'

"Sir, I have been asked to accompany you to the viewing area. I can assure you; I will keep you safe. Please follow me." She doesn't wait for a response and I have to jog a little to catch up with her as I want to grab my jacket before leaving. After a few minutes of walking down mysterious corridors and listening to incomprehensible chat on a walkie talkie, I find myself safely sat behind Katherine with my security detail next to me, gun drawn beneath the wooden shield.

In the candle lit hall with camera crews swarming around the tiny central table, two greats of Yorkshire meet for a chess duel. A very, very rare event. Jonathan is taller than I had imagined him. He is clean shaven and is wearing an open neck black shirt and black trousers. He looks like a trombonist at a school jazz band. Katherine does not stand for him and so they shake hands once they are both sat.

"It's a pleasure to see you again Jonathan."

"The pleasure is all mine." Jonathan replies in a deep husky voice.

The official who had told me to stop tapping my foot approaches the table and turns to face the cameras. He is a short man with an afro. He has a warm smile which makes him perfect for television.

"Since we are in the final match and the winner of the contest is yet to be decided. A flip of the coin will be used to decide which player will play white or black." He turns to the contestants, First Minister Hyde, would you call it?"

"Tails." Jonathan declares as the coin flips in mid-air. The official reveals the coin on his forearm.

"It is heads. First Minister Tyne, would you like to play black or white?"

"White, thank you." Katherine appears calm and composed but the colour hasn't quite returned to her cheeks. The official makes a big ceremony of rotating the chess board around as initially Katherine had sat behind black. Humility pays dividends. I think of Archbishop Sentamu.

To chess experts, the game that was played by these two is incredibly famous and only attempted by the very best. It is an imitation of a game played by Bobby Fischer against Boris Spassky in 1972, Iceland. In game 8 Spassky had made a famous blunder when playing an English Symmetrical game. Katherine must believe she has thought it through and knows how to cope with Fisher's set up. It is a good job she did because the game unfolded exactly as Fischer had played it. Jonathan has done his homework.

I spy Muhammed sat on the benches behind Jonathan. He gives me a little salute and I smile in return. Annoyingly a camera has picked up our exchange and so we both look back to the table and pretend nothing has happened. The game seems destined for a draw. I hope Katherine has thought this through. We need a win, not a rematch.

Forty-five minutes pass with an even share of pieces going to Katherine and Jonathan. Each player has a solitary rook and an even number of pawns. The interesting aspect of the board comes down to pawn position. This is the point that I suddenly understand the game plan. Jonathan has four pawns, two are diagonally connected whereas his other two are isolated individuals in no-man's land. Similarly, Katherine also has four pawns however, they are all diagonally connected to form a protective barrier around each other on the left side of the board. Meanwhile, Katherine's king hides in one of the gaps between her pawns. Jonathan's king is standing in the open near the right-hand side of the board. Away from Katherine's pawns.

Over the next ten minutes Katherine manages to pick off the two independent pawns leaving Jonathan with two. Then, it a moment of great courage, Katherine forces the swap of rooks. Its pawns only now. Jonathan rapidly tries to bring his King across to neutralise the danger, but the damage has been done. With Katherine's King providing additional protection to her pawns, the writing is on the wall.

Jonathan is a man of great pride. He never resigns, he waits to be put into checkmate. There is always a chance of a stalemate. Katherine would have researched this and so she carefully and methodically entraps Jonathan's king in a maze of pawns, always making sure to keep him in check. She manipulates his King into the prime position so that when the pawn reaches the end of the board and turns into a queen, it also brings with it checkmate.

Muhammed stands. I stand. Cheers can be heard coming from the streets. A mixture of emotions could be viewed on the faces of officials and stewards. Katherine and Jonathan remain motionless. Eventually, after what feels like hours of celebrations in my mind, and to be honest pure relief, Jonathan rises from his chair.

"Look after York well." He bows to Katherine and then begins to applaud. The Minster erupts into scattered applause echoing around the great building.

"Let the people in!" Katherine booms from her chair. The ceremonial guards on the main door heed her words immediately and the great oak doors creak open. The noise levels double. Flags and banners could be seen in the street outside and then a stampede of footsteps came towards the Minster. Megaphones reminded people to remain calm and thankfully there were no injuries.

The Yorkshire Rose with a red N which I had admired on entry is now one of thousands of flags. Katherine had done it. We have won back our land. We have won back our people. I let out a cheer and tears well in my eyes. Before long I am picked up by strangers and hugged.

Viva La Revolution. I hear the chant of Yorkshire... Yorkshire... and a few of the crowd make my fist sign that I had used in my video against Claire. We are superheroes to these people.

Chapter Thirty Three: Walking the Walls

Little did I know, Hannah has actually planned a victory parade route. Apparently she didn't want to tempt fate and let us know. It is a simple outline, nonetheless, walking the walls of York. Legend says they were originally built by the conquering Romans, so Hannah wants us to appear like conquerors. It takes us a long time to get there! Crowds of supporters swarm the Minster and Katherine is actually carried out by the crowd to roars of applause.

I knew there was a lot of support for North Yorkshire, but I am a little dubious about the extent of the celebrations. I want to see where the East Yorkshire loyalists have gone. We still have to successful pass the transition period for York to be ours. Jonathan and Muhammed disappeared from the viewing benches in a flash. As soon as I exit the building I see hints of East Yorkshire, a flag with Yorkshire Rose defaced with a Red E has been set on fire above the courthouse. No doubt East Yorkshire TV journalists are recording this and insinuating that this was an insurrection by scoundrels and hooligans.

If you have been at a football stadium when the game is over, that is the extent of confusion I am surrounded by. I saw Hannah take a phone call about ten minutes ago and now she is somewhere in the crowd, nowhere to be seen.

Thankfully the crowd realise that swarming over the walls themselves would be a recipe for disaster and they make way for me to walk up without impediment. I find Katherine looking out at the train station below with a huge smile on her face.

"I want to thank you Rowan." She says without looking at me. Honestly! She can change her mood so quickly! It wasn't that long ago that she was berating me in that tiny interview room in Castle Howard. Although to me it feels like months with all my brother's problems.

I decide to play along with feigned humility. "Thank me for what? You are the one who claimed the victory!" Neither of us are looking at each other. We just stare at the beautiful city which will soon lie in North Yorkshire jurisdiction.

"You know exactly what I am thanking you for."
She begins to grimace and looks me in the eye.
"But before we celebrate too heavily I have to
warn you about something. I have heard some
rumours…"

Before she can finish her thought I get a tap on the
shoulder from a panic-stricken Hannah, phone in
one hand whilst she obsessively pushes her other
hand through her hair. I think she may well be
having a panic attack.

"Hannah are you alright? Here, just perch against
this bit of wall and I'll try and find you some water."
I look around inquisitively to see if any supporters
might just happen to be carrying a bottle of some
sort.

"No… no… Rowan listen to me." Hannah says
between exaggerated breaths. "It's Rosanna!"

Katherine looks guilty.

"What do you mean Rosanna? She hasn't replied
to my email has she?" I ask with a touch of hope.

"She submitted a challenge against you the
moment Katherine won." Hannah turns and throws

up over the wall. I hear noises from angry people below who had been vomited on.

All of a sudden I feel like I am walking under water. Katherine pats me on the shoulder and murmurs something about trying to negotiate with her and then she leaves to meet with cooing journalists desperate for her attention.

Hannah continues to recover, perched against the wall. She must feel responsible for Rosanna's decision.

"Tell her I accept for tomorrow afternoon at two o'clock. Make sure I get table 14 in the chess hall." I put on a fake smile to reassure Hannah and then go to meet my adoring fans.

Chapter Thirty Four: Emotions

I am actually extremely annoyed. Trust Rosanna to time her challenge like this. She knows exactly what she is doing, she is attempting to catch me off guard, as I have just had a major success, she is hoping to use my concoction of emotions to hinder my decision making. Well, I will not rise to it. She is like a teenage girl trying to annoy her older brother.

I do not want to kill Rosanna. I want to make that clear in my official record. If all goes to plan she will agree to work with me once more. I have a sneaking suspicion this challenge is more of a cry for attention and a personal attack than actually about duelling. Let us not forget, Rosanna has never been a skilled chess player. She scraped a pass in her basic chess exams.

I had a few drinks last night but drank with moderation to avoid any problems this morning. Obviously we have no data on how Rosanna plays, so Hannah and I sit on the couch and hypothesise how she will play and what her real motives are. Generally, beginners play with a King's pawn opening and if they are completely incompetent they play with a flank opening (moving the pawns in front of the rooks). I have a suspicion that a King's pawn opening is likely and so I focus my attention of dealing with standard play.

We eat lunch like kings. The octagon has been flooded with baskets of fruit and other assorted gifts. We use the free-range eggs gifted by a farmer to make Eggy-Bread and enjoy reading the morning papers which talk of our huge success and the jubilant celebrations across York all night. Apparently the local government has never been so popular within North Yorkshire.

Hannah has managed to keep my duel under wraps although I doubt anyone would have paid attention anyway with all the other stories in the news. In fact, all the journalists must have been redeployed elsewhere because when we arrive at Castle Howard there isn't a soul in sight. Autumn has begun and fallen brown leaves are scattered across the cobbled stones. Hannah and I stride across to the main door where Katherine is awaiting us.

Reception has been redecorated, huge Yorkshire flags have been draped over the bannisters and the red carpet has been replaced with royal blue.

"When did all these updates occur?" I ask Katherine on entry and look around the corridor.

"We had a crack team update it over the last fortnight. I am glad to see you relaxed! I was worried you would be insufferable this morning."

"I think this is more of a negotiation than a real challenge. Besides, chess was never Rosanna's forte, you remember that right!" I say with confidence although there is a sliver of concern in my mind. I do remember Rosanna making some inciteful comments about Katherine's win over Esther. I am hoping this element of doubt will sharpen my senses in case I do actually have to play.

"She has been here for an hour already. She looks serious to me."

Katherine walks towards the steps, before reaching the foot of the stairwell she hesitates. "I have something to confess. I tried to say something yesterday, but the time wasn't right."

Hannah steps out, leaving the room to Katherine and I. "You once said to me that there is no such thing as a right time or place when something important needs to be said!"

Katherine continues, "Rosanna approached me months ago about her concerns. She and Professor Odoi wanted reassurance that you couldn't use the NSSRIs to your advantage permanently. That is why I tried to pressure you to provide access to East Yorkshire sooner. The professor was uncomfortable with the political situation and felt you wouldn't listen to him. He said you had been corrupted with power."

I am dumbfounded by the treachery. Everyone seems to have been in on this little conspiracy. Despite everything I have done for this county! "Something tells me there is more." I fold my arms and I scowl at Katherine. I feel like my eyes could burn a hole in Katherine's side.

"Yesterday morning. I was late because I had organised a meeting with Rosanna. She informed me of her plans. I gave her my blessing. You are not the eagle-eyed young councillor you once were. Rosanna is right, power and success have changed you." I look away and begin to walk towards the chess hall.

Katherine continues, "I am telling you this now because I have every confidence that you will successfully negotiate with Rosanna if you just put your ego aside and listen. She was your strongest asset. Don't let her go."

I feel drunk with anger. I am surprised I can walk straight. I see Rosanna at table 14. She is the only person in the hall apart from Hannah who is talking to the camera man. She is trying to persuade him not to record, a subtle trick we sometimes use to avoid media scrutiny. It looks like Hannah has struck a deal as the camera is pointed away from our table.

Rosanna is wearing her duelling dress, Yorkshire Rose emblazoned over the front. Except there is a subtle difference. She has sewn, with red thread, a N through the rose. She is wearing my symbol; I feel sudden relief. This is a clear sign that Rosanna wants back into the fold.

I take my seat and before I can say a word the official comes across.

"I see your challenger has arrived." He says addressing Rosanna, he must have been so bored watching her sat alone for an hour in here. "Standard rules apply. Ninety minutes each." He starts my clock and leaves. I had completely forgotten that I play white when I have been challenged. I have spent the morning preparing for Rosanna's opening move and yet I am the one opening!

I play the King's pawn opening. Keep her in the game so we can have a chat.

"Do you remember Callum and Paul's match?" Rosanna hasn't looked at my opening move. She stares unblinkingly at me.

"Of course, I do. I miss him every day."

"Liar. You have clearly forgotten but before he died he asked to speak with me. He whispered something in my ear. You never asked me what he said. Would you like to know?"

"Sure, I'll bite." I feel offended by Rosanna's insinuation that I didn't care about Callum, but I recognise she has some anger to let out before we can negotiate.

"He said: Rowan is an amoralistic monster. We both know, North Yorkshire needs Rosanna Halewood in office." I swear Rosanna still hasn't blinked. "Those were his last words, Rowan."

"It is your move." Is all I can say. I am really hurt and part of me doesn't believe her.

She moves her King's pawn forward. I move my Queen's pawn forward. Centre game established. She takes the pawn. Centre game accepted. I am thankful the camera isn't on me. I am sweating buckets and feel like I could cry.

"Professor Odoi thinks you're a selfish bastard. He calls me regularly to vent his concerns about the thousands in need of our pill. Hundreds dying across the world every day. When was the last time you called him?" Rosanna's style of confrontation is grating on me and I can't hold it back.

"Alright Rosanna what is this? We both know you're a pathetic chess player. Are you planning on shouting at me for a while and then negotiating a truce or do you just want to say your piece and then let me kill you? Your plan has already failed, camera crew isn't paying attention. Everything you say is just between us, you can't defame me to the public."

"I couldn't defame you if I tried. You're invincible in the public's opinion. I am here to kill you, make no mistake. As soon as I left the Octagon that day I learnt who you are. You are Jonathan Malenkovic, except you have power and some semblance of good political sense. You are selfish and manipulative. I am ashamed to have enabled you. The only way I can repair the damage I have done to my country is to remove you from it."

I move my bishop out into the board. She replies swiftly with a knight. "You see my dress. I am a true supporter of North Yorkshire. You are a supporter of yourself."

I cannot take it anymore. I stand up and flip the table. Pieces scatter everywhere. The cameraman cannot ignore this and swivels the camera towards me. "How dare you! I am King's Piece of North Yorkshire. I am the political mastermind of the NSSRIs. I am responsible for York's return to North Yorkshire. Pay me some respect."

Rosanna smiles. The moment I see her lips move I realise what she has done. "I realised you hadn't read the chess rules in depth when we were talking about East Yorkshire in the Octagon."

"You evil woman... You Jezebel!" I blubber. I look around the stone floor, littered with chess pieces.

"A player cannot disrupt the board intentionally during a duel. Any deliberate attempt to disrupt play will be deemed an automatic forfeit." Rosanna quotes from her mind.

"She is correct councillor." Says the official who has run across. "You are to come with me. I hereby declare Rosanna Halewood victorious. You are sentenced to death under Act 7 of the Geniocracy code of conduct."

"Oh, and if I am Jezebel… You are Ahab." Rosanna states.

I do not wish to recount any further. The torrent of abuse that I directed at Rosanna is not how I want to be remembered. Since my death is imminent I know there is no need for me to be honest about what happened after that. Who is going to prosecute me? Rosanna is sat with her gun in the room next door.

As my last statement I would like to say this. Serving as councillor for North Yorkshire has been the honour of my life. I am sure Rosanna will do everything she can to ruin my reputation, but I am proud of my achievements. I took a risk with mental health reform, it paid off. I made mistakes letting success get to my head and similarly, I paid the price. Life is made up of peaks and troughs. Those who are most successful are the ones who do well in the troughs.

My love to North Yorkshire. Never give up the struggle, we have come so far. We are truly God's own county.

Chapter Thirty Five: Alternative Views

I, Rosanna Halewood, declare the following account to be honest and true to the best of my recollection. I will do my utmost to keep my account in line with government guidelines under the 2091 Reliable Witness and Justice Act. I swear I will not conceal any information, nor will I fail to record any meetings or conversations which are of any significance in my life.

I have not slept a wink. I seem to move between a state of incredibly intense chess research and productivity to the polar opposite state of wallowing in bed at the overwhelming sadness which covers me like a cloak. I still can't quite believe what I am about to do, but whenever I weigh it up in my mind, I know this is the right decision. I have to kill Rowan or die trying.

My panic disorder has been debilitating over the past week, but I cannot face taking Schofield's tablet, I can't stomach it. I am finding myself trembling and drinking so much water to deal with my dry mouth that I am going to the toilet every twenty minutes. I am having to take breaks from chess preparation to cry and do breathing exercises. I just sit on my rocking chair, hands on my knees breathing deeply and trying not to vomit. Panic attacks are terrible and debilitating. What would I have been if I wasn't mentally unwell?

The doctor told me it would take some time for my previous medication to kick in again. I stopped taking my SSRI pills because Schofield's tablet was better. I started them again last Monday and have made it past the initial nausea, now just waiting for them to reduce my panic symptoms.

I am pleased with how far my chess has come. I didn't learn properly in school. My mum was convinced I would challenge someone and die which would leave her all alone. She said that if I never learnt I would never be tempted to put myself in such a dangerous position. I agreed not to try too hard but I recorded all the lessons so I would be able to learn in future if I ever wanted to. Young Rosanna was wise! They have come in handy.

However, I have no intention of winning at chess. I have every intention of winning via the by-laws. I need just enough chess ability to look competent. To make Rowan think I have learnt something.

I eat a solitary slice of buttered toast for lunch but can't manage any more.

I arrive early to prepare. I have always been in the business of arriving early. There is an advantage to be gained just by being comfortable with your surroundings, whatever you are trying to achieve. I had guessed Rowan would request table 14, we have history here. I take his normal seat to at least make him slightly less comfortable. I also want him sat facing towards the camera so the world can see his reaction. If everything goes to plan there will be quite a reaction!

The chess hall is stunning and, when you are not working with someone famous, no one bothers you. You can sit peacefully and absorb the ambience. The most amazing aspect of Castle Howard is the grounds. When I was a little girl, I often dreamed of being proposed to in the gardens. Sadly, romance in my life died a death when I married my work. I had suitors but I am grateful that I didn't do what Callum did and get married anyway, he was miserable until the very end.

The official comes over two or three times to tell me I am welcome to take a walk or get a drink as I am an hour early, but I respectfully decline his offers. I want to be settled. I want to be part of the furniture, immovable. I spy Katherine pacing in the foyer, but I don't make any attempt to acknowledge her, I imagine she is panicking about backstabbing Rowan. She was a little apprehensive in our meeting yesterday, so I was expecting her to try and backtrack.

When Rowan arrives, he looks tired. I thought my challenge would stop him partying too hard last night, but he seems to have enjoyed at least some of the festivities. He is stubbly as normal, but his piercing green eyes appear dulled and distracted. He swaggers over to the table with confidence, but I detect hints of anger in his manner.

The official is relieved that my opponent has finally arrived. I think he felt awkward about having me on his turf. Time to play, time to talk.

"Do you remember Callum and Paul's match?" I ask with as much intensity I can muster. He seems taken aback that we are already discussing things of such emotional power.

"Of course, I do. I miss him every day." He says with the emotion of a sociopath.

"Liar." He flinches at this word. Excellent start. "You have clearly forgotten but before he died he asked to speak with me. He whispered something in my ear. You never asked me what he said. Would you like to know?"

"Sure, I'll bite." Who does he think he is? A dog? Now it is my turn to become the liar.

"He said: Rowan is an amoralistic monster. We both know, North Yorkshire needs Rosanna Halewood in office." No, he didn't. "Those were his last words, Rowan." No, they weren't. His last words were actually: Make sure my kids are always OK. I am grateful that I can use this angry manner as anger is a fantastic way to hide panic attacks. People think you are shaking with rage when you are really shaking with fear. I can feel a dry mouth coming on.

He is angry but nowhere near the anger I saw in him on my last day in the Octagon. I need to layer more insults on and lay them on thick. We play one of the openings I read about in my book last night. I know how to play the next few moves but need to keep him talking before we get into unfamiliar territory.

"Professor Odoi thinks you're a selfish bastard." This is true which means I feel like I can say it with more venom. I haven't sworn in years and the power of the word gives me a little thrill. "He calls me regularly to vent his concerns about the thousands in need of his NSSRIs. Hundreds dying across the world every day. When was the last time you called him?"

I see his lips purse. I've hit a nerve now. Need to keep the intensity up. I don't have much more knowledge of how to play chess from this position. "Alright Rosanna what is this? We both know you're a pathetic chess player. Are you planning on shouting at me for a while and then negotiating a truce or do you just want to say your piece and then let me kill you? Your plan has already failed, camera crew isn't paying attention. Everything you say is just between us, you can't defame me to the public."

This outburst is a strong indicator that I am near the intended mark. When I worked with Rowan the only times he became nervous and guilty was when he had to execute someone. I have thought of the perfect name to invoke to push him over the edge. Jonathan Malenkovic, the similarities between him and the person Rowan has become are striking.

"I couldn't defame you if I tried. You're invincible in the public's opinion. I am here to kill you, make no mistake. As soon as I left the Octagon that day I learnt who you are. You are Jonathan Malenkovic, except you have power and some semblance of

267

good political sense. You are selfish and manipulative. I am ashamed to have enabled you. The only way I can repair the damage I have done to my country is to remove you from it." I say this with enough umph to make him fear me for the first time. To make him see me as his equal, or even is better. I certainly have taken the moral high ground.

I must keep plugging away at him, at every opportunity. I scramble in my mind for other ideas, "You see my dress. I am a true supporter of North Yorkshire. You are a supporter of yourself." This has tipped the scales. I see it straight away. I have taken something he is truly proud of, his childish North Yorkshire symbol, and used it against him.

In a flash he is on his feet and then, to unimaginable relief I see chess pieces join him at head height. I've done it. He has taken the bait. I feel a smile pushing my lips apart, I can't stop if it even if I wanted to. It's a strange feeling, I am so happy and yet I am suspecting I will be challenged by a citizen in a matter of days. Rowan Schofield is a national idol, and I have acted as his judge, jury and executioner. No one will ever believe that Katherine was involved.

I decide to explain my smile to him, although I think he has already realised this was my plan all along, "I realised you hadn't read the chess rules in depth when we were talking about East Yorkshire in the Octagon." He is muttering insults like a toddler who has lost his toy to his older sister. He calls me Jezebel. I call him Ahab. We are as bad as each other, and soon enough we will both be confined to the history books. Both having been killed.

Officials are by my side and declare my victory. They escort the blubbering mess to the execution office across the yard. I watch him through the window being dragged, feet trailing on the cobbled stones. The great politician has fallen so far.

I unstrap my gun from my hip and take deep breaths. I knew there was a possibility that my scheme would work. I knew this moment may come. After everything we have been through together, killing him will be the ultimate betrayal. I think of my Dad. I pray. I see Katherine walk in through the corner of my eye. She says nothing but embraces me. I know what she is implying, I have a legal duty. I have a moral obligation.

I walk slowly across the courtyard. Cars are racing to the scene over the hills, journalists have heard the news and are putting their lives at risk to get here in time. I will not let them see this. As a parting gift to Rowan, this will always remain between us. I enter the execution office.

Rowan took it bravely I must say.

Chapter Thirty Six: Why

I imagine, of all the entries into my journal, this moment will be the most visited in the future by historians and journalists alike. Most will be viewing this account to investigate the reasons for the betrayal of my former boss and close friend. Some will see me as a hero, others as a villain. I write this from my mini, parked in my driveway after killing one of my longest friends. I feel devoid of life. Am I Judas?

As you are no doubt aware, I am only required to keep a log of my daily activities from my 18th birthday. The reasons for doing what I have done lie in events that took place in my childhood and therefore one cannot find them unless you search my parents accounts. I have reason to believe the events that changed the course of my life are not in my Dad's accounts and my mother had a completely different perspective on the matter. Therefore, I will attempt to record it here, despite the pain it brings me to think of it.

At thirteen years of age, I recognised that my Father had been suffering with depression for a few years. We lived on a farm in Killinghall, a village outside Harrogate which had undergone significant development prior to the revolution and so farming communities had lost a lot of their land to housing developments. We were one of the worst hit by the changes, losing half of our livestock as we simply had no place to put them.

My Dad became more and more unwell. Getting up to milk the cows was pretty much all he did for a year or so, he employed farmhands to take over the running of the farm whilst he rested in bed and watched the same TV shows on repeat for months on end. He said he found them comforting, reminded him what life could be like. I tried so many times to emphasise to him that sitcoms do not reflect what actual people are like, that they are scripted friendships. He couldn't take it; he thought his relationships were pathetic in comparison. He cut out friends because they didn't 'treat me with the respect of a true friend.'

For a year or so I thought his problem was believing everything he saw on TV. It wasn't until my mum finally convinced the doctor to come round that he explained that these were symptoms of an underlying illness called depression. He gave him some tablets and left. The same tablets I now take.

To be fair to Dr Collingwood the tablets did make my dad more active. He began to resume some of the farm duties he had done when I was a kid. No one was more grateful for his return than Jesse our sheep dog who had been somewhat neglected in his absence. There was something still off about him, however.

To distract from the problem, I threw myself into my schoolwork which is how I met Rowan. He was competitive and managed to beat me at tennis on our first meeting, but I bested him at other events, especially in music. He was a good friend to me, we used to meet in the park with our friends and talk. His drive to be the best gave me the passion I needed to pursue my work. If it wasn't for him I doubt I would have made it to university. And now I have killed him.

When I turned fifteen I finally put my finger on what was wrong with Dad. He had no emotion anymore, he was numb. I only recognised this when I overheard an argument between Mum and Dad about how to treat a farmworker who had been late on a few occasions. My Mum felt that he should be given another chance, we didn't know what might be going on in his life, my Dad just said he didn't have time to investigate everyone's homelives and had to run a business.

It was bizarre to hear my Dad talk in this way when it was not so long ago that he was bedbound because of his own emotions. Mum phoned Dr Collingwood again but he said this was just a result of the tablets that he was on and it was a sacrifice he had to make to keep my Dad out of bed.

My Dad killed himself two weeks later.

I found him in our barn with cows standing over him as if to hide the tragedy from me. He had taken an overdose and sat in the barn amidst the mooing to prevent anyone hearing him be sick. So that no one could get him help. He left a note, it read:

My dearest Rosanna,

I love you with all my heart. I hope you will never forget that.

Many will call me a coward for doing what I have done. I doubt they would have said the same thing if I had killed myself because I had motor neurone disease, Huntington's disease or some other chronic condition ruining my life. Mental health doesn't matter to other men. We tell each other to stop being a wimp.

I had a chronic condition, never let anyone deny this, and its name was depression. I pray that one day some doctor somewhere will be able to help people like me. However, I know it will not happen in my lifetime, so I have taken the easy way out. Look after your mum and the farm. But, Rosanna, you are destined for great things, never give up on your dreams,

Love Dad

The pain was unbearable. Suicide is such as selfish act, he left us with nothing. He ruined my university years and made me a damaged woman. Damaged goods with a wound that never seemed to heal, and no doctor could see the extent of my pain.

When Rowan approached me and asked if I would be his pawn, I was not inclined to take the offer. However, when he mentioned his mental health plan I was persuaded. I thought of all the other little girls in the world who would lose their loved ones to this terrible disease.

I hope you understand, whoever is reading this. I hope you see now. Let's pretend for a second that I had grown up in South Yorkshire and there was a tablet that would save my Dad's life in North Yorkshire that he couldn't get access to. How is that fair? Or imagine my Dad was one of those people whom the NSSRIs do not help, but no one is looking out for him. Would my Dad have been the man who poured red paint on Rowan? How many lives will I save my getting rid of Rowan and giving this tablet to the rest of Yorkshire, the rest of the world even.

The ends justify the means. I know history may not look kindly upon me. I know many will wonder what else Rowan could have done given another ten years in power. No one will ever be able to count the lives I will have saved. No one will ever understand the extent of what I have done, for the good of the people. For the good of my people. For my Dad.

The ends justify the means. I'm sure they do.

The End.

Afterword

I hope you found this account interesting. I have used many aspects of these accounts to illustrate my point that Rosanna was a hero, not a villain. Personally, the most compelling aspect is the comparison of Jonathan Malenkovic as a challenger with Rowan Schofield's last chess match. The arrogance and self-confidence are so similar. I feel Rosanna was right in her assessment of Rowan, despite popular opinion that she was simply a disgruntled former employee.

As we know Rosanna was killed in a matter of weeks by a challenger loyal to Schofield. She was not a great chess player, but my goodness did she know the by-laws. Katherine opened up the supply chain of Schofield's pill on Christmas day 2123. How long would Councillor Schofield have kept NSSRIs in North Yorkshire only? Thousands if not millions of lives have been saved as a result and many more have had their quality of life drastically improved. Who should be given credit for his success? I submit to you that Councillor Tyne,

Schofield and Halewood should all be held in equal esteem for this great accomplishment.

Kaley Abrahams

Printed in Great Britain
by Amazon

67429802R00166